SAVING JENNA

BROTHERHOOD PROTECTORS YELLOWSTONE
BOOK SEVEN

ELLE JAMES

TWISTED PAGE INC

SAVING JENNA

BROTHERHOOD PROTECTORS
YELLOWSTONE BOOK #7

New York Times & USA Today
Bestselling Author

ELLE JAMES

To my sister who is always up for a little brainstorming.
Love you!
Elle James

CHAPTER 1

AFTER CHECKING IN AT THE NURSES' station on the third floor, Jenna Jenkins hurried to the room number she'd been given. She knocked lightly on the door.

"Jenna?" a soft, familiar voice called out.

Jenna pushed through the swinging door and entered the room. The lights were muted, but there was no mistaking the face of the woman lying against the stark white sheets, her ginger hair fanned out on the pillow behind her.

"Brittany, sweetie." Jenna rushed to her bedside and wrapped her arms around her younger half-sister as best she could without disturbing the IV attached to her arm.

"Oh, Jenna," Brittany clung to her, her arms thinner than the last time she'd seen her almost a year ago.

A lump rose in Jenna's throat. She swallowed hard. "Oh, baby, what happened? Why are you here?" She leaned back. "Are you hurt? Sick? Tell me. What's going on? When did you get in town?"

Her sister gave her a weak smile. "A couple of weeks ago."

Jenna frowned. "You've been in Bozeman for a couple of weeks?" She shook her head. "Why didn't you let me know?"

Her sister shrugged. "You have your own life." She glanced down at the IV in her arm. "I didn't want to bother you with mine."

Jenna's heart squeezed hard in her chest. "You're never a bother, Brittany. Never. I love you."

A tear rolled down her cheek. Brittany brushed it away. "Yeah, well, I love you, too. And that's why I didn't want to bother you with the mess I've made of my life. I'm twenty-six years old. I should've figured things out by now." She waved a hand around the room. "Instead, I dropped out of college and have bounced around from one dead-end job to another." Her voice faded. "And one worthless boyfriend to another."

Jenna touched a finger to Brittany's chin and raised her head until she was forced to look at her. "You're still my sister. No matter what. You can always come to me. You always have a place to go. I told you that a long time ago."

Another tear rolled down her cheek. "I know. But you're so...so...together. You have your degree, a great job with the FBI and a guy who makes you happy."

Jenna snorted. "I'm not as together as you think. Ryan and I broke up almost a year ago."

Brittany's brow creased. "Oh, Jenna, I'm so sorry."

"It's okay. We dated for five years, and he never made a move to make it permanent. I finally told him to shit or get off the pot."

Brittany's eyes widened. "You didn't."

Jenna nodded. "I did. And he got off the pot. He's since met his soulmate, married and is already expecting a baby. He's happily married. I'm happily single. It's all good." Though she made light of it, Ryan's quick rebound after breaking up with her had hurt more than she'd admit.

She still wondered what was wrong with her that he hadn't been able to commit to her after five years but could commit to the new girlfriend after only a few months...?

"But look at you," Brittany said. "You've still got it together."

"What other choice do I have?" Jenna sighed. "Life goes on."

Brittany nodded. "Yes, it does."

Jenna tipped her head toward the IV. "So, what brings you to the hospital? Kidney stones? Ruptured appendix?" She prayed it wasn't anything more serious like the leukemia that had claimed their mother. She held her breath, waiting for Brittany's answer.

Her sister glanced away. "I made a mistake moving in with Larry."

Based on her sister's judgment in men, Jenna wasn't surprised. Now wasn't the time to say that. "How so?"

"He wasn't who I thought he was."

"I thought you said he was a pharmaceutical salesman."

Brittany met Jenna's gaze. "Oh, he is that, but I thought I was his one and only." She snorted and looked down at her hands. "I found out those long stretches where he was away weren't just to make sales. He was going home to Salt Lake City to his wife and kids."

Jenna's jaw hardened. "That bastard." As more tears flowed down Brittany's cheeks, Jenna took her hand. "At least you found out before it went too far."

Brittany's fingers curled around hers. "That's just it…" She met Jenna's gaze. "Things went too far."

Jenna's brow dipped. "What do you mean?"

The swinging door pushed inward as a nurse backed in, pulling a cart through. She wore her hair in a thick braid twisted into a tight knot at her nape and covered with a hair net. "Miss Berry, it's dinner time," she announced.

"That's Nurse Grey," Brittany said.

Jenna cast a brief glance at the older nurse and returned her attention to Brittany. "Your dinner can wait a moment. What do you mean *things went too far?*"

Brittany's lips quirked on the corners. "My dinner can wait, but hers can't." She nodded toward the woman entering the room as she slowly spun the cart to reveal a clear plastic container.

A soft mewling sound grew louder. Movement inside the container made Jenna's breath catch in her throat. She straightened and turned fully to look into what she now recognized as a hospital bassinet. Inside lay a tiny baby cocooned in a tightly wrapped blanket, its face turning dark pink as it revved up the volume from mewling to full-on crying.

Jenna looked from the crying baby to her sister. "I don't understand."

Brittany laughed. "It's a baby. Jenna," her sister paused, "meet your niece."

The nurse gathered the baby from the bassinet and carried it to Brittany, placing the infant in her mother's arms.

Mother.

"You're a mother?" Jenna struggled to process this information, though the evidence was as clear as the baby in her sister's arms. "But how?"

Brittany's lips twisted. "Really?" She adjusted her hospital gown, exposing a full breast. The nurse helped her adjust the baby's position, pressing her face to the distended nipple.

At first, the infant didn't seem to know what to do, but then its little lips latched on.

Brittany sucked in a sharp breath.

"It might hurt at first, but before long, you'll get used to it," the nurse reassured her with a smile. "And mother's milk is best for your little one." She straightened. "I'll be back in a few minutes to check on you."

"Thank you," Brittany said.

When Nurse Grey left the room, Brittany fussed with the baby. "She hasn't quite got the hang of this yet." Finally, she looked up, her brow furrowing. "Aren't you going to say something?"

"Why didn't you tell me you were pregnant?"

"Things were on-again-off-again with Larry. We had our fights and made up so many times. I thought it was normal and that I was handling it without help from my big sister. We were pregnant. A baby would make it all work." She lifted a shoulder and let it fall. "Until I found out he was married."

Jenna shook her head. "Every time we talked…"

"I know. I should've told you then. But the timing never seemed right. It seems like every time I think I get things right, they fall apart. I wanted to handle this on my own."

"But this isn't a rent payment or a new set of

tires." Jenna waved a hand toward the bundle in her sister's arms. "It's a baby. A lifetime commitment."

Brittany's brow dipped lower. "I know. I should've told you, but it's complicated."

Afraid to ask, she did anyway. "How complicated?"

Brittany bit her bottom lip. "When I confronted Larry about the fact he was married, I asked him if he was going to leave his wife and kids." She snorted. "He said no. I asked him if he planned on helping me support our child. He said no. When I asked how he expected me to support the baby, he said he expected me to give it up for adoption."

"Bastard," Jenna whispered between clenched teeth.

Brittany stared down at the baby girl in her arms. "After he drank a six-pack of beer, he passed out watching a football game. I packed my bag with what little I owned, took some money from Larry's wallet and walked out. I drove to the one place I had any family...Bozeman. You were my backup plan."

"You didn't call me."

"I couldn't," Brittany whispered. "You've bailed me out too many times already. I had to figure out this mess on my own." She sighed. "Only I think I made it worse."

Jenna dropped into a chair beside the bed, unsure she could handle more of Brittany's drama.

Her sister continued. "I took a temporary job as a bartender only because the guy who owned the bar also rented me a garage apartment. He knew I didn't have much money and that it wouldn't go far. On top of that, my car quit working. He felt sorry for me and let me work a few hours a day. It wasn't much, but the tips helped."

Jenna thought back over the past couple of weeks. How long had it been since she'd talked with her sister? She usually called every other week. Had it been longer? What kind of older sister was she if she didn't check on her sister more often than once a month?

Brittany shifted the baby to the other breast and helped her latch on before continuing. "Anyway, I realized that working at a bar and living in a tiny garage apartment that was smaller than a college dorm room wasn't going to cut it. But I couldn't afford anything else. I was feeling desperate. The baby was almost here, and I couldn't support it."

Jenna started to say something.

Brittany held up a hand. "I know I should've called you., but I didn't. My mistake. I was working at the bar when a man came in and sat at the bar. He asked for a rum and coke. While I fixed it for him, he asked me when my baby was due. We talked for a while. He seemed nice. I confided that I was thinking of giving up my baby for adoption, so it could have a better life than I could provide."

Jenna's heart sank. "What did you do?"

Brittany stared at her sister, her eyes filling with tears. "He told me he and his wife had tried to have children, but after five miscarriages and one live birth that ended in the baby dying from SIDs, they'd given up. They lived in a big empty house. He made plenty of money to raise a dozen children and send them all to college without taking out a loan."

"Money isn't everything," Jenna said.

"That's easy to say when you have it," Brittany said. "But it wasn't just the money. He said he loved his wife so much and wished he could give her the baby they both wanted so badly. They were exactly what my baby needed to make it in life. A happily married couple able to give my baby the life I couldn't."

Jenna knew where this was going, her heart sinking into the pit of her belly. "You told him he could adopt your baby?" Her gaze rested on the sweet baby girl pressed against her mother's breast.

"I made him give me a copy of his driver's license and a copy of his savings and investments statement. My boss at the bar had a cop buddy run a background check on the guy. He was a legit, upstanding citizen in the community with no criminal record. His wife was a volunteer at the local food bank. I drove by the address he gave me, the same one on his driver's license. It was a big, beautiful house with a huge yard. I couldn't give my baby any of that."

Jenna would have helped, but she held her tongue and let her sister continue.

"I agreed to let him adopt my baby, knowing it would be the best life for it. I was fully prepared to hand it over." She stared down at the baby, suckling at her breast. "Until she finally made her appearance." Brittany's lips curled into a soft smile. "Once I held her in my arms, I knew I'd do anything to make her happy. Anything but give her up." Brittany looked up and caught Jenna's gaze. "He paid a lot of money to help with my expenses when I couldn't work the last couple of weeks. I owe him a lot." She shook her head. "But I can't give him my baby."

Jenna pressed a hand to her tight chest, thankful she'd gotten to her sister before the man showed up demanding the baby he'd bought and paid for. "We'll pay him back."

"I have no money," Brittany said.

"I do," Jenna offered. "I put back some money for a rainy day." At that moment, no rainstorm was as important as keeping Brittany and her baby girl together. "We'll figure it out." She patted her sister's arm. "Together."

Tears slid down Brittany's face. "I really tried not to rely on you. I want to be able to take care of myself and my child. I just can't right now."

"That's what family is for," Jenna said. "We take care of each other." She wrapped her arms around her sister and the baby and hugged them gently, tears slipping down her own cheeks. "And no more secrets. We have to work together to make a good home for the baby." She gave a short laugh. "Does she have a name?"

Brittany shook her head. "I didn't want to give her one if I was going to give her up for adoption. Now... I don't know."

"I always liked the name Olivia," Jenna offered.

"I like it," Brittany glanced down at the baby with a light orange fuzz across her scalp. "I've always thought Brenna or Blakely were good names."

"Blakely." Jenna nodded. "I like it." She looked down at the baby and smiled. "It's a good name for a little spitfire like her mother." She gently feathered her fingers over the baby's fuzzy scalp, her heart already swelling with love for her niece.

"Blakely Berry," Brittany rolled the name on her tongue. "I think we have a name. Don't you, sweetheart?" she spoke softly.

The nurse returned. "Do you need help with the baby?"

Brittany shook her head and smiled at Jenna. "I have my sister to help."

"I'm headed out for the night," Nurse Grey said. "Angie Smalls will take the night shift if you need anything. She'll come to take the baby back to the nursery when you're ready to sleep." She turned to Jenna. "I take it you're Miss Berry's sister?"

Jenna nodded, too shocked to form words.

"They brought Miss Berry in so quickly I'm sure there's paperwork to sign in admissions. Now would be a good time to take care of that while the baby is feeding."

"Yes, of course." Jenna stood.

"Goodnight, ladies," Nurse Grey said with a smile.

"Goodnight, and thank you," Brittany said. "For everything."

"Congratulations, Miss Berry," the nurse said. "She's a beautiful baby."

A younger nurse entered the room. "Oh, Lena, you're still here?"

Nurse Grey nodded. "Just on my way out. I need to get home to make sure Mama gets her meds."

"How is your mama," the young nurse asked as she took the baby from Brittany and laid her in the bassinet.

Nurse Grey's lips pressed together. "She doesn't remember me at all."

"Nurse Grey's mother has Alzheimer's," Brittany said.

"I'm so sorry," Jenna said. "It has to be hard."

Nurse Grey nodded. "No one really prepares for this—mentally or financially." She shrugged. "Life is full circle. She cared for me when I couldn't care for myself as an infant and child. It's my turn to care for her when she can't care for herself. Speaking of which...I'm outta here."

The older nurse left.

"Do you want me to take the baby to the nursery?" Nurse Smalls asked.

"Not yet," Brittany said. "I want my sister to get to know her a little better."

"Buzz me if you or the baby need anything. I need to check on the other new mothers." Nurse Smalls left the room.

"I have to run by admissions first," Jenna said. "Will you be awake long enough for me to get there and back?"

Brittany yawned again. "I will."

Jenna shot a worried glance at Brittany. "Will you be all right alone with the baby?"

Brittany draped an arm over the side of the bassinet and stroked the baby's cheek. "I'll be okay. She's asleep. I can stay awake until you get back. I want you to get to know your niece before we descend on your little cottage."

Jenna hadn't thought past the idea that she had a niece to even consider taking her sister and the baby home. Her little three-bedroom-one-bathroom cottage had been all she'd needed when she'd come to live there and had taken the job of regional agent for the tiny FBI outpost.

The addition of one more adult and an infant... well, they'd just have to make do. Jenna wouldn't say no to her sister and the baby in their time of need.

No matter how many times she'd bailed Brittany out of financial and relationship disasters, she was the only family she had left. Her lips lifted as she stared down at the tiny baby. Okay, so now, Brittany and her baby were the only two members of her family she had left.

"I'll hurry," Jenna promised and slipped out of the room, letting the door swing closed softly behind her.

Angie Smalls, carrying a Styrofoam cup with a straw, turned a smile her way as she entered a room several doors down from Brittany's.

Jenna passed a slim young man wearing a gray maintenance coverall with a hospital ID card dangling from a clip on his pocket. He carried a wad of sheets to a large canvas laundry basket on wheels and dumped them inside before ducking into one of the rooms.

A heavily pregnant woman in a hospital gown and bright yellow hospital-issue socks leaned against a man as they walked the length of the hallway. She stopped, curled her arm around her huge belly and bent over. "That was a good one."

The man glanced at his watch. "The contractions are coming faster. Not long now." He rubbed her back a few times and whispered, "Have I told you how beautiful you look?"

She snorted, the sound cut off as she doubled over

again. "Yeah, right," she hissed. "Shut up and get me back to the room."

"Yes, ma'am," the man said with a grin.

Jenna shook her head. Delivering a baby wasn't for the faint of heart. Based on the woman's expression, the pain was significant.

Brittany had gone through labor and delivery without someone she knew and loved. She couldn't blame her for wanting to keep her baby girl. After nine months carrying her and a traumatic delivery, she had to have developed feelings for the little being.

Jenna took the elevator down to the first floor and stopped at the admissions desk, where she filled out paperwork, wondering how much having a baby cost. Since Brittany didn't have a job and wasn't one to think too far ahead, Jenna would bet she didn't have insurance.

She signed the papers and squared her shoulders, knowing she'd be the one to wade through the bureaucracy to get the baby covered under Medicaid or any option available until Brittany could find a job or go back to college or a trade school.

Whatever choice Brittany made, she couldn't go off half-cocked. She had a baby to consider. Her days of being a rolling stone were over.

Jenna shook her head as she headed for the elevator. She wasn't sure Brittany would rise to the challenge of being a mother to that sweet little infant, which meant her big sister would have to make sure the baby was cared for properly. They'd also have to come up with the money to pay back the man who'd funded Brittany during the last weeks of her pregnancy.

In the meantime, Jenna had to get her home ready for Brittany and her infant daughter. Didn't babies need a lot of stuff like a crib, diapers, bottles and so much more?

Jenna's gut clenched. More than likely, she'd help Brittany care for the babe. She wasn't ready to take on a newborn. What did she know about babies?

Nothing.

Holy hell. Her simple, single life just got a whole lot more complicated.

Back up the elevator to the third floor, Jenna breathed in and out, willing her heartbeat to slow before she had a full-blown panic attack.

Having an infant in her house would take some getting used to, but she could do it.

As the elevator reached the third floor, Jenna drew in a deep breath and let it out slowly. The doors parted, and she stepped out.

The hallway was empty except for the janitor in the gray coverall at the far end, pushing a large yellow mop bucket through the door to the stairwell.

Jenna pasted a smile on her face and strode toward Brittany's room. She could do this.

They could do this.

Together.

Before she reached the door, it swung open.

"Help!" Brittany clung to the door, blood dripping from a wound on her temple. She spotted Jenna and lurched toward her. "Help! Oh, dear God. Help!"

She fell into Jenna's arms.

Jenna staggered backward, taking her sister's full weight. "What's wrong?"

"My baby," Brittany cried. "He stole my baby!"

Jenna's heart thudded against her ribs. "The baby?" She steadied Brittany and held her at arm's length. "Where's the baby?"

Tears streamed from her eyes. "The janitor. He came into my room while I was in the bathroom. When I came out, he was leaning over the bassinet. I...I asked him what the hell..." She shook her head from side to side. "He grabbed my dinner tray and came at me...and hit me." She touched a hand to her temple, coming away with blood. "I fell, but he kept hitting me. I...must've blacked out. When I got up, he was gone..." Brittany stared into Jenna's eyes. "And so was my baby. You have to catch him."

Jenna remembered seeing the janitor pushing a mop bucket through the stairwell door. She hadn't seen the man's face. "What did he look like?"

"I don't know. One moment he had his back to me, and the next, he was pounding me with the tray."

"Was he young? Old? Facial hair?"

"I...I..." Tears slipped down Brittany's cheeks. "Can't remember. Maybe a mustache? I mostly

17

remember the tray coming at me. Then he was gone." Her breath caught. "With my baby. Go after him!" Brittany pushed away from Jenna. "Go before he gets away."

She swayed and would have fallen if Jenna hadn't stepped forward and wrapped an arm around her. "I can't leave you like this."

"I don't care about me," Brittany cried. "Save my baby!"

Angie Smalls, the nurse on the night shift, emerged from a room down the hallway, a frown creasing her brow. "What's going on?" She rushed forward. "What are you doing up?"

"Did anyone come to collect my sister's baby?" Jenna asked, hoping Brittany was wrong and this was all a mistake, though her gut told her it wasn't.

Angie shook her head. "I didn't. She said she wanted to keep her in the room a little longer." Her brow dipped. "Why?"

"She's gone," Brittany sobbed. "He took her." She pushed away from Jenna. "Find him. Find my baby." When she staggered backward, the nurse slid an arm around her.

Jenna met the nurse's gaze. "Take care of her. I'm going after the man who took the baby."

"I'll call security. They'll lock down the hospital until the baby's found." Angie, hampered by supporting Brittany's waist, moved toward the nurses' station.

Jenna ran to the far end of the hallway and burst through the door. The janitor had a head start on her. Would it be too much of a lead for her to catch him before he left the hospital?

She didn't know, but she did know she had to try. Her baby niece's life depended on it.

CHAPTER 2

"MAN, I appreciate you getting me to the hospital when you did," August Walsh's head lolled on the pillow, his words slurring slightly from the effects of the anesthesia and pain medications. "I mean, you had better things to do than take me for emergency surgery. Will your new boss be put out when you show up late?"

Cliff Cranston shook his head. "I called Stone while you were in the OR. He's fine. Showing up a day late won't make a difference. He doesn't have an assignment for me at the moment. I'd just be twiddling my thumbs or looking for ways to get in trouble if I have nothing else to do. So, you're saving me from giving Stone a bad first impression."

Gus closed his eyes and sighed. "I've been shot, hit by shrapnel and thrown from a vehicle. None of that hurt like those gallstones."

"I've heard women say it's worse pain than giving birth," Cliff said.

"Remind me not to give birth to kidney stones," Gus said, his voice trailing off. For a long moment, he was silent.

Cliff walked to the window overlooking the parking lot below, feeling caged by the walls around him.

"Dude, you don't have to stay," Gus said.

Cliff turned to face him. "I told you I don't have anywhere else to be."

"I'm just going to sleep." Gus frowned. "For that matter, I can have someone from the Brighter Days Rehab Ranch come get me when they release me tomorrow. No use sticking around watching my IV drip."

Cliff's lips twitched. "I don't mind," he lied. He'd rather be anywhere than in a hospital. The only other times he'd been in hospitals were when someone was dying. His dad died of a heart attack in a hospital. His mother went in for a routine hysterectomy and died of an aneurysm.

His best friend had died in a hospital after their last mission in Syria. That situation had been in a field hospital where he'd been taken to be stabilized prior to medical evacuation back to Ramstein, Germany. Only Dutton hadn't stabilized. He'd bled out before they could plug all the holes from the IED that had blown shrapnel through him.

"Seriously," Gus said, closing his eyes again. "You got me here. Now, leave. You're making me nervous."

"Why?" Cliff asked.

"Because I'd be nervous if I were in your shoes." He raised his free hand to push his hair off his forehead. "I hate hospitals. I can't imagine you like them any better. Go to West Yellowstone. Start your new job. You got me this far. I can make it the rest of the way without your help."

"Brighter Days knows you're here in Bozeman," Cliff said aloud, more for himself than Gus. "Hannah, the physical therapist, said she'd head to town to check on you in the morning."

"See?" Gus met and held Cliff's gaze. "You have no reason to hang out here. Unless you're afraid of moving on to your next career. Maybe you're just as in need of therapy for PTSD as I am. In that case, stay and check yourself in to rehab at Brighter Days."

Cliff's eyebrows drew together into a V over his nose. "I'm fine."

"Yeah. So you say." Gus lay back against the pillow. "Prove it. Go to West Yellowstone. Join the Brotherhood Protectors. Save the world you couldn't save back in Syria."

Gus's challenge was like a giant fist gripping his heart, squeezing so hard his chest hurt. There was more truth in Gus's words than Cliff cared to admit.

"Okay," Cliff finally said. "I'm going. I'll call

Hannah at Brighter Days and let her know she'll need to get you back to the ranch."

Gus sighed. "Good. I might finally get some rest."

Cliff laughed. "You're an asshole."

Gus grinned, his eyes remaining closed. "And you're a dumbass, making me jump through hoops to get you to leave me in peace."

"You have your cell phone on the nightstand. If you need anything…don't call me," Cliff said.

"Damn right," Gus said.

Cliff strode to the door and glanced back. "I hope you feel better soon," he said.

"Love you, too, sweetcakes." Gus's chuckles followed Cliff out the door.

He started to turn toward the elevator, caught sight of a nurse wheeling a patient, bed and all into the elevator and opted for the stairs.

He could use the exercise. They'd driven from San Diego to Bozeman in two days. If Gus hadn't had the gallstones, he would already be processed into the Brighter Days Rehab Ranch, and Cliff would be in West Yellowstone with Stone Jacobs and his team of Brotherhood Protectors. Cliff wasn't disappointed at the delay. He'd taken Stone's offer because it was the only one he felt even remotely qualified for.

Since leaving high school, the only job Cliff had was the Navy. Being a Navy SEAL, making it through BUD/S training and then performing dangerous missions all over the world had been his life.

Then why the hell had he left?

He'd asked himself that a hundred times and came back to the same answer.

Because he'd lost too much. His friends, brothers in arms, people he'd give his life to save if he could. He'd lost pieces of himself when a particular battle ended in collateral damage, a bullshit way of saying civilian casualties, like women and children. And he'd lost his conviction that he was fighting for his country.

Then there was the PTSD thing. For so long, he'd thought Post Traumatic Stress Disorder was a copout. People just needed to pull themselves up by their bootstraps and get on with life.

Yeah, he'd had nightmares and flashbacks after certain battles that hadn't gone quite according to the plan. For the most part, he'd pushed past them, and they'd faded. Until Syria.

Until the village filled with regular people only trying to get by in a war-torn country. Old men, women and children going about their lives.

Then the explosion.

One minute the sun had been shining. A small child carrying a rag doll had stepped on what appeared to be a small mound in the dirt.

Cliff's heart raced, beating so fast it hurt. Sweat broke out on his forehead, and he trembled from head to toe.

Damn. Not now.

Before the panic attack rendered him catatonic, Cliff pushed through the stairwell door and dove through, slamming into someone on the other side.

The other person flew backward and hit the wall. Unable to slow his momentum, Cliff crushed the unsuspecting person.

Together, they slid down the wall to the concrete landing.

The shock of plowing into someone else arrested the panic attack and cleared his mind of the images of that day in Syria. He struggled to untangle himself from the other person's arms and legs and rolled to the side, nearly tipping over the edge of the landing onto the stairs leading downward.

When he turned to the person he'd bowled over, he realized it was a woman. She sat with her back to the wall, her eyes wide and a hand pressed to her chest.

"I'm so sorry." Cliff knelt on the floor beside her. "Are you okay?"

She shook her head and mouthed the words, *Can't breathe.*

"Jesus." He leaped to his feet. "I'll get help."

As he turned, he heard her gasp.

"Oh, thank God," she said.

He turned back. "Are you going to be okay while I get someone to help?"

She shook her head. "No time." Her hand reached up. "Help me up."

"Are you sure that's a good idea?" Though he wasn't certain she should be getting up after being hit harder than a linebacker going after the quarterback, he gripped her hand.

"Wasting time." She took his hand and pulled herself to her feet. "He's getting away." As she stood, she swayed and nearly fell.

Cliff pulled her into his arms and held her until she was steady on her feet.

Her hands planted on his chest, and she pushed him back. "He can't get away. Have to catch him."

Afraid she'd fall, he held on.

"Let go of me." Tears welled in her eyes. "Please."

The tears made his chest tighten. "You'll fall."

"A chance I'll take." She broke free and turned toward the stairs leading to the floor below.

He gripped her elbow. "You're not steady enough. Take the elevator."

She shook his hand off and started down, her knees buckling.

Cliff stepped down beside her, slipped an arm around her waist and held her up. "If you're going down, at least let me help."

"Hurry." She took another step.

His feet moved to match hers.

After a few more steps, she seemed to regain her balance enough to increase her speed. "I can do this on my own," she said. "Have to go faster."

He dropped his arm from around her waist but

ran down the stairs beside her to the bottom floor.

As she burst from the stairwell, she looked right then left.

Right appeared to be toward the lobby. Left led toward the rear of the hospital. She turned left and ran.

Afraid he'd knocked her senseless, Cliff ran after the woman, surprised at how fast she moved.

At the end of the hallway, they could turn right or left. She chose right and ran.

A sign over the door at the far end read EXIT.

As they neared, a security guard stepped through the door and frowned at them. "Stop."

"Let us by," the woman called out without slowing.

He shook his head. "The hospital is on shutdown. I can't let you out."

"But you have to let me out," she said, coming to an abrupt stop in front of the man.

"I can't. There's been an incident. A baby was taken from labor and delivery. No one goes in or out except through the front entrance and only after the police release them."

The woman reached into her back pocket and pulled out a wallet, displaying a badge. "I'm Special Agent Jenkins with the FBI. Let me pass."

"Ma'am," the security guard crossed his arms over his chest, "I don't care if you're the President of the United States. My orders are to guard this exit with my life. No one goes in or out. I repeat, if you want out of the building, you'll have to go through the front entrance."

"You don't understand," Special Agent Jenkins said. "The man who took the baby could be getting away as we speak. I have to stop him."

"Lady, the city and state police have this place surrounded. If the guy is still in or around the hospital, he's not getting away."

Special Agent Jenkins stared at the man a moment longer, then spun on her heels, pushed past Cliff and ran.

She obviously didn't need his help anymore to keep her steady on her feet, but he followed, his curiosity getting the better of him and because he'd been responsible for slowing her pursuit of the kidnapper.

When they emerged into the hospital's front entrance, it was full of uniformed officers, both city and state police. Everyone seemed to be talking at once, and four officers stood guard at the door, barring anyone from entering or leaving.

Jenkins frowned, planted her hands on her hips and looked around the room. Her gaze landed on a group of men, some in uniform, some in plain clothes, and she marched across the floor.

Cliff followed, stopping far enough away not to interfere but close enough to hear what Jenkins was saying.

"Chief Bryant." She glanced from him to the other men standing around. "Who's in charge?"

"Special Agent Jenkins," the man with gray hair and a Bozeman City Police uniform nodded toward her. "I didn't know the FBI had been notified. Unless the child was airlifted from the hospital grounds, it couldn't possibly have crossed state lines. Until that happens, this case isn't in your jurisdiction. It's not your business."

The Special Agent nodded. "I understand it's not in my jurisdiction. However, it's very much my business. That baby is my niece. I want to know everything about this case. I want my sister's baby back. ASAP."

"We all want that baby back, but you have to let us handle it. In the meantime, I have a detective talking with your sister. If you have anything to add to her report, I suggest you go to her. No one's leaving the hospital until it's been searched top to bottom, and everyone has been screened and questioned—including you."

"But he might already be off hospital grounds," she said, looking past him to the guarded doors. "I need to be out there, looking for him and the baby."

"We have a BOLO out and roadblocks on every major road leading out of Bozeman."

"And if he's on foot?" she demanded.

The chief shook his head, his stern gaze softening.

"You're one person. We have many out there looking."

Jenkins glanced to the corners of the room. "What about video surveillance cameras?"

"I have a detective reviewing footage as we speak. You're welcome to join him..." the stern look returned, "as long as you don't interfere."

The agent's jaw hardened. "That's where I'll be."

"Your sister might need a relative to be with her at a time like this," the chief suggested.

"I'm the only relative she has...besides her baby. I'm sure she'd rather I found my niece than hold her hand." She looked around. "Where do they keep the videos?"

The chief crooked a finger at one of the uniformed officers standing nearby. "Show Special Agent Jenkins to the security office."

Jenkins turned, noticed Cliff standing there and frowned. "You don't have to follow me. I'm not going to faint or anything."

"I know," he said.

She followed the uniformed officer.

With nothing better to do, Cliff followed her.

At the doorway to the security office, the uniformed officer left Jenkins and returned to the front lobby.

Several men crowded around an array of monitors replaying footage from all over the hospital, concentrating on labor and delivery.

With no additional room for Jenkins to join them, she watched from the doorway.

"You're still following me," she said softly.

"I feel bad for knocking you down in the stairwell."

"You should. You slowed me down. I could've been out of the hospital before the security guard blocked the exit."

"I'm sorry," Cliff said.

Her eyes narrowed. "Why did you run into the stairwell?" Her back stiffened. "Where were you coming from?" Eyes widening, she poked a finger at his chest. "Was it you? Did you take my sister's baby and hide it somewhere on the second floor?"

He held up his hands, backing away from her and the room full of police detectives. "I didn't take the baby. I was here for a friend who had emergency gallbladder surgery."

She advanced on him, poking her finger into his chest again. "Then what were you running from if not the police?"

He hesitated, heat rising into his cheeks. "Nothing."

"I don't believe you." She glanced over her shoulder toward the security office. "I think the police need to interrogate you." As she turned, he reached out and grabbed her arm.

"Okay," he said. "I was running. But not from anyone. And I didn't take the baby."

She gave a pointed stare at the hand on her arm. "I'm not buying it."

He released her. "I wasn't running from anyone. I was running... I was having..." Cliff swore under his breath. "I had a massive panic attack. I dove through that door so people wouldn't see me lose my shit." He pushed a hand through his hair, turned away for a moment then faced her again. "Look, I'm sorry about your sister's baby. If there's anything I can do to help, I will. If I hadn't stopped you when I did, you might've caught up to him."

Her frown deepened. "Panic attack?" Her gaze swept over him. "You don't strike me as a man who has panic attacks."

"Yeah, and I'd appreciate it if you'd keep it to yourself." He drew in a deep breath and let it out slowly. "It's not something I'm proud of."

She planted a fist on one hip. Her dark brows rose, and moss green eyes challenged. "Why should I believe you?" Jenkins wore no makeup and didn't need to. Naturally dark lashes framed moss green eyes; her pale smooth completion required no enhancements. She was a naturally beautiful woman —and appeared to be as tough as nails. She had to be strong and confident to make it through the FBI academy.

Cliff had to admit he was impressed and maybe a little attracted to a woman who could stand up to men in a male-dominated career field.

"You shouldn't believe me." His lips twisted. "I wouldn't believe me if I were you. Until the baby is found, you shouldn't trust anyone."

Her lips quirked on the corners. "At least we agree on something." She tipped her chin toward him. "Where were you before you ran into me in the stairwell?"

"In my friend's room," Cliff said. "He's recovering from surgery."

"Can he vouch for your whereabouts?"

"As long as they haven't given him any pain meds to help him sleep. Not that he'd ask for them."

"Tough guy?" she quipped.

He nodded. "One of the toughest."

"And you're not?"

He shrugged. "I am when I need to be."

Her frown softened a little. "Chemical imbalance? Or trauma?"

Cliff frowned. "Huh?"

"The...you know..." she lowered her voice, "panic attacks?"

"Not important," he said. "What's important is finding your sister's baby. And I meant it. If I can help in any way, I will."

"Like you can drop everything and go on a manhunt? Don't you have a job?"

"I do, but I can postpone my start date."

"Start date? You haven't started this job? And your new boss is okay with that?"

"Should be."

Jenkins snorted. "I need a boss like that. What is it you do that you can put off so easily?"

"I'm going to work for an organization called the Brotherhood Protectors."

The agent's brows rose. "Hank Patterson's bunch?"

He nodded. "Heard of them?"

"I have. They're making quite a name for themselves in these parts. They saved one of our Special Agents and shut down the terrorist training camp she exposed." Jenkins grinned. "She married Hank's guy...Kujo, I think, is his name. Has a retired military working dog. Last I heard, he mated with a wolf."

"Kujo?"

Jenkins rolled her eyes. "No. The dog." She squinted, looking down her nose at him. "I guess you can't be all bad if you're going to work for Hank." Her brow dipped. "From what I understand, he only hires former military, special operations types. Is that what you are?"

Cliff raised a hand. "Guilty. Navy SEAL. I'm going to work for the branch in West Yellowstone, not Eagle Rock."

She nodded. "You wouldn't think in a state with as low a population as Montana that we'd need so much help protecting our citizens. Then again, there's a lot of territory to cover and not enough law enforcement personnel to go around."

"Are you saying you want me to help you find that baby?"

"We should leave it to the local and state authorities to do their jobs."

He cocked an eyebrow. "And you're going to leave it to the local and state authorities?"

"Absolutely," she answered. "Although, this abduction could fall into my ongoing investigation into the disappearances of young Native American women in this area. *Pregnant* young women."

Cliff ran his gaze over Agent Jenkins. Her hair was dark enough, but her features and green eyes didn't necessarily appear Native American. "Are you and your sister Native American?"

She snorted. "Not even close. Brittany is a strawberry-blonde with pale skin."

"You two don't look much alike."

"The only thing we have in common is our mother's green eyes," she said. "I have *my* father's black hair. We're half-sisters. My mother remarried after my father died."

Voices rose inside the security office.

Special Agent Jenkins and Cliff leaned in to find a man pointing at one of the screens. "There. Back that one up several seconds."

The security guard manning the computer slowly backed the video to an earlier time. As he did, a figure in a gray hospital maintenance coverall and ball cap walked out onto what appeared to be a loading dock, pushing a large, rolling canvas basket into a waiting delivery truck.

Jenkins moved closer. "That could be the janitor I saw mopping on the labor and delivery floor when I went to see my sister and her baby."

The man beside the security guard held out his hand. "Detective Schwope. You're Special Agent Jenkins, our local FBI representative, aren't you?"

Jenkins nodded. "I am. The baby taken was my sister's."

The detective's lips pressed together. "I'm sorry this is happening to you both." He turned back to the monitor. "Were you there when the attack occurred?"

"Unfortunately, no," she said. "I went down to admissions, and when I came back, I saw the janitor go through the stairwell door as I got off the elevator. I thought nothing of it until my sister staggered out of her room, calling for help."

"And that's why you were running down the stairwell when I ran into you," Cliff said quietly behind her.

Her fists clenched at her sides. "I didn't run after him soon enough. I couldn't leave my sister until a nurse came to help me with her."

The detective sitting beside the security guard had the guard zoom in on the side of the truck until he could clearly read the company's name. He pulled out his cell phone and called a number. "Chief, have your guys on the streets look for an EZClean delivery truck, medium-sized, white with green lettering on the side." He ended the call and slipped his cell phone into his shirt pocket.

"Who has access to the doors leading to the delivery dock?" Jenna asked the guard softly.

"Security and anyone with a maintenance badge," the guard said, his fingers flying over the keyboard.

"Check the badges used on that door at that time," Detective Schwope said.

"On it," the guard said. A list popped up on the monitor directly in front of him. He scrolled down until he got to the time corresponding to the man loading the bin into the truck at the dock. He leaned forward and read the name aloud, "Robert Whitley." He pulled up another screen. "He's not even assigned to the night shift. He's not due to come in until five thirty in the morning."

"Any other maintenance personnel leave right before the hospital went on lockdown?" Jenkins asked.

The security guard returned to the list of cards scanned during that time and shook his head. "No maintenance staff, except for Whitley. But we had a shift change of nursing staff around that timeframe."

"We need to track them down and question them," the detective said. "Even if they didn't take the baby, they might have seen something or someone suspicious."

Jenkins nodded. "Is that all you found on the

videos?"

"Just the laundry truck and the nursing staff shift change," the security guard said. "The nurses usually leave through the front entrance. None of the fire exits were used, or we would've been alerted."

"What about the third-floor footage," Jenkins asked.

The security guard pointed to a black screen. "For some reason, the camera went dark around that time."

"Did you see the janitor in the footage before it went dark?" Jenkins asked.

"Briefly." The guard backed the images up to a time thirty minutes before Brittany was attacked. He sped through the thirty minutes as Nurse Grey moved in and out of rooms, pushing a chart cart or carrying cups of water to the patients. A hugely pregnant woman walked the hallway in her hospital gown with her husband at her side.

At high speed, the people moving about appeared comical. Cliff's lips twitched.

Then came a janitor in a gray coverall, wearing a ball cap. He worked his way down the hall, pushing a dust mop. He disappeared through a door at the end and reappeared with a big yellow mop bucket, backing down the hallway, stopping to spot-mop as he went. Never once did he turn to face the camera.

At one point, he pulled a cleaning rag out of his pocket and wiped at a spot on the wall. The next moment, he disappeared beneath the camera. Moments later, the screen went dark as if someone had placed a curtain over the camera.

"I'll go through the footage one more time to see if we can catch the janitor with his face toward the camera on one of the other floors," the detective said.

Jenkins nodded, pulled out her wallet and handed the detective her business card. "If you find anything else, I'd appreciate it if you'd share it with me."

He nodded. "I'm sorry about your sister and her baby. I have a couple of kids of my own. I can't imagine someone stealing them from me."

Special Agent Jenkins gave the man a tight smile. "Thanks," she said and turned for the door.

"Jenkins," the detective called out.

The agent turned. "Sir?"

"It goes both ways." He pulled a business card from his pocket. "If you find anything, we'd appreciate your sharing. The more people we have on the case, the better chance we have of finding the baby."

Jenkins nodded. "Deal." She tucked the detective's card into her wallet and left the security office.

Cliff followed. "Where to?"

"*I'm* going to see my sister. I want to hear her account of the attack again. After that, I'll check in with the chief and the detectives to see how the questioning is coming along. We might be stuck in the hospital for a while."

He walked with her to the elevator.

She pushed the button and glanced his way. "You don't have to come with me, you know."

"What else do I have to do?" he said. "Besides I—"

"—feel responsible." She shook her head. "Don't you need to check in on your friend?"

"I will."

The elevator door opened.

Jenkins stepped in.

Cliff stepped in beside her. "After we see your sister. I feel fully invested in this investigation."

The FBI agent touched the button for the third floor and cast a frown toward Cliff. "You're not a member of the city or state police and shouldn't be mucking around in this case."

"And it doesn't appear as if the state or local police have invited the FBI to assist with the investigation." He crossed his arms over his chest. "You shouldn't be mucking around in this case."

"It's my niece."

"And I could've killed you by slamming into you in that stairwell. I feel responsible. And I take my responsibilities seriously."

She stared into his eyes. Most women had to look up a long way to meet his gaze.

Agent Jenkins was taller than most women and didn't have to tilt her head back nearly as much to look him in the eye. "Fine," she said. "Just don't get in the way."

"Yes, ma'am," he said and nearly leaned down to

claim her full, rosy lips. He caught himself halfway there and straightened.

What the hell was he thinking?

Obviously, he wasn't thinking at all. Had he kissed the woman, he was sure she'd have knocked him on his ass. And since she worked for the federal government, would kissing her be considered a federal offense?

His gaze swept over her mouth.

It might be worth going to federal prison for one kiss. He faced the elevator doors, his lips twitching.

"What's so funny?" Jenkins demanded.

"Nothing," he said and glanced at his watch. "I just realized we've been together for almost an hour now, and I don't know your first name."

She snorted. "I've got you beat," she said. "I don't know your first or last name."

He turned to her and held out his hand. "Cliff Cranston. Nice to meet you."

Jenkins took his hand, her lips quirking on the corners. "Special Agent Jenkins."

Cliff frowned as the elevator door opened and Jenkins stepped out.

"Seriously?" he asked.

She turned just enough that he could see a grin slip across her face. It disappeared as quickly as it had appeared.

That brief transformation from serious profes-sional to playful young woman stopped Cliff in his tracks and made his blood race through his veins, heading south to his groin. Before he could collect his thoughts and follow her, the elevator doors started to close.

Cliff stuck his hand through the gap, causing the doors to open again, and he stepped out.

Why he continued to follow her, he wasn't sure. Or the reason was one he wasn't willing to admit to himself.

Whatever the reason, he couldn't walk away. He had to see where this case was going. And maybe, after they found the baby, he'd see where anything else between him and the FBI agent would lead.

A voice in the back of his head that sounded a lot like Gus said, *Dude, don't get ahead of yourself.*

Cliff ignored the voice. It was too late, anyway. Jenkins intrigued him, and he couldn't walk away when her baby niece was missing.

He was a member of the Brotherhood Protectors. Well, almost. What had Stone Jacobs told him about the organization? They were there to protect, rescue and extract people from difficult situations when law enforcement or the federal government weren't quite enough, couldn't handle it or needed a hand.

Helping Special Agent Jenkins find her niece fit the Brotherhood Protectors' mission statement.

Now, to convince Jenkins he'd be an asset, not a hindrance.

Yeah, he had his work cut out for him.

CHAPTER 3

WITH CLIFF CRANSTON, a former Navy SEAL, following her like a needy puppy, Jenna hurried back to Brittany's room and tapped lightly on the door before entering. She didn't want to be too loud if her sister was asleep.

When there was no response, Jenna eased open the door. The sound of voices flowed out into the hallway.

A state police officer and a plain-clothes detective stood on either side of Brittany's bed while Nurse Angie (or Smalls!) stood at the foot of her bed. They barked questions at the young mother while Nurse Angie shot daggers at them with her eyes and tried to get to her patient to adjust the IV and check her vital signs.

"Brittany?" Jenna called out.

"Jenna!" Brittany's head lifted off the pillow, her eyes round and worried. "Did you find—" When her gaze took in Jenna's empty arms, she sagged back against the pillow, tears slipping down her cheeks. "She's gone, isn't she?"

Jenna glared at the men. "Out," she said calmly, softly, emphasizing the command with her gaze and the tightness of her lips.

"But—" the state police officer started.

"If you haven't asked all the questions by now," Jenna said, "they'll have to wait until morning. Miss Berry needs rest."

When the detective opened his mouth to say something, Jenna raised her chin and narrowed her eyes at the man. He clamped his mouth shut and closed the pad he'd been writing on. As he turned to move away, Brittany grabbed his arm. "Please, find my baby."

He patted her hand awkwardly and said, "We'll do our best."

Brittany released her hold, letting her hand drop to the bed beside her. "Please," she whispered, the sound choked by a sob.

Once the men left Brittany's bedside, Nurse Angie recorded Brittany's vitals and asked, "What's your level of pain?"

"Ten out of ten," Brittany said. "My heart is broken. I can barely breathe because my baby's gone."

"Do you want me to give you something to help you sleep?" Nurse Angie asked.

"No." Brittany swiped at the tears on her cheeks. "How can I sleep when my baby is missing? She's so little. So fragile. I don't even know if she'll survive. What will she eat? Who will take care of her? Will they be kind to her? The man who took her came at me violently, hitting me over and over after I was already down. He was so angry. Will he take that same anger out on my baby?" She pounded her fist against the mattress. "I don't know what's happening to her. It's killing me."

"Brittany, honey," Jenna said softly, closing the distance between them, "let Nurse Angie give you something to take the edge off."

Her sister stared at Jenna. "Is this punishment for all the years I've been a pain in the ass? Is this karma coming back to spit in my face?" She bit her bottom lip. "If I'm to be punished, punish me. Not my baby." Her shoulders shook with silent sobs as a torrent of tears drenched her face.

Jenna nodded to Nurse Angi. "Give her something to help her calm down."

"No." Brittany sucked in a shaky breath. "I need to stay awake. I need to be alert if they bring her back to me."

"You need to be healthy and rested *when* she comes back," Jenna insisted. "You're making yourself sick by staying awake and crying so much."

"I can't stop," Brittany said. "For once in my life, I know what I want. I want my baby. And I promise I'll be a good mom to her. I'll go back to school, get a degree then get a job so that I can provide everything she needs. She deserves a good life. Not the crappy excuse for living I've been doing since high school. Please," she pressed her fist against her lips. "Please let her come back to me. I didn't even have a chance to name her. She's out there somewhere, and she doesn't even have a name on her birth certificate." More tears flowed.

"What did you tell the detective?" Jenna asked.

"I told them everything I told you," she answered.

"About the baby's father and the man who wanted to adopt her?"

"They said they'd send someone to check on Larry and Mr. Waters." She closed her eyes. "Please let her be with one of them. Although why Larry would want a baby when he has another family, I don't know. And I hadn't told Mr. Waters anything about changing my mind." She raised her hand to her battered face and winced. "Why did he hit me so many times after I was down? He was so angry he wouldn't stop. Oh, God. My poor baby is with that monster." Her body shook with silent sobs.

"Sweetie." Nurse Angie touched Brittany's arm. "I'm going to give you something to help you. I promise, when your baby is back, I'll make sure you're awake and ready to take care of her."

Brittany blinked back tears. "Promise?"

Angie gave her kind smile. "Promise."

Brittany lay back against the white sheets, her strawberry blond hair a tangled mess, her bruised face blotchy and damp. "Do it," she whispered. "I can't stop imagining the worst. My poor, sweet baby."

Nurse Angie added a syringe full of something to the IV. "That should help," she said softly.

"The only thing that will help is for whoever took my baby to bring her back safe and sound." Brittany's voice faded.

"Sweetie," Jenna leaned close. "Before you sleep, do you have the phone number of the man who gave you money for you to live on during your pregnancy.

"Shhh," she said, her words slurred, her eyes mostly closed. "Big secret. His wife doesn't know. He wanted to surprise her."

"I'll need his phone number so that I can tell him that you don't want to give him your baby. That the deal's off. It might be easier if I did it."

"Would you do that for me?" Brittany's damp eyes opened, luminous and rounded. "Or are you only playing big sis coming to the rescue? Or is the super intelligent sister, who has everything she ever dreamed of, baling out the screwup once again?"

Jenna took her sister's free hand and squeezed it gently. "You'd do it for me."

Brittany raised Jenna's hand to press a kiss to her

knuckles. "I don't deserve you, Jenna. I don't know what I'd do without you."

"Well, you don't have to find out. You're stuck with me for a very long time," Jenna said her eyes filling. "And Baby Blakely is stuck with Auntie Jenna."

"She'll love you as much as I do," Brittany said.

Jenna sank into the chair beside her sister's bed, still holding her hand.

Brittany's eyes narrowed. "Uh, Jenna, there's a man behind you. Tell me you know him and that you'll introduce him to me." She brushed the tears from her cheeks and finger-combed her hair. Leaning her head toward Jenna, she whispered, "He's super cute."

"I heard that," Cliff said with a grin.

Jenna chuckled. "Brittany, this is Cliff Cranston. I met him in the stairwell a few minutes ago and can't seem to shake him."

Brittany glared at Cliff. "Do you want me to chase him off?"

"No, sweetie," Jenna said. "He's going to help me find your baby."

"Do you even know him?" Brittany demanded, her frowning gaze pinning Cliff.

"Not really," Jenna said, shooting a glance over her shoulder at Cliff, standing back from the bed, close to the door, as if preparing for a quick getaway.

Brittany's jaw dropped. "My sister, the FBI agent, inviting a complete stranger to help her solve a case?"

"When you put it that way, it makes me sound like I'm too stupid to live. Cliff's a former Navy SEAL. They have top-secret clearances and have been entrusted with missions involving national security around the world. I think we can trust him."

Her frown fading as her eyelids lowered, Brittany said, "Did he show you his secret handshake, frog tattoo and ID card? What proof?"

Jenna cocked an eyebrow toward Cliff. "Well?"

"I can show you the ID card they gave me to use in the VA's medical system. Since I left before retirement, I don't have an active or retired ID." Cliff reached into his back pocket, pulled out his wallet and extracted his VA medical ID card. He handed the card to Jenna, then shrugged off his jacket and pulled the hem of his T-shirt from his waistband.

"Whoa. Wait." Jenna's heart leaped, her pulse ratcheting. She raised her hand. "What are you doing?"

"Showing you my frog tattoo." Before she could stop him, he pulled off his T-shirt and turned around so that she could see his back.

Her breath lodged in her throat at the broad expanse of muscles and the array of colorful tattoos etched across his skin. On his left shoulder was the skeleton of a frog. Besides the tattoos, several large and small scars were scattered across his left side and back.

Jenna forced air into her lungs, her pulse still hammering. "He has the ID," she whispered.

"Good," Brittany murmured. "Tattoo?"

Jenna shook her head. "Does the skeleton of a frog count?" Her gaze met Cliff's.

A shadow crossed his face.

"Yeah," Brittany said. "Real...deal..." Jenna glanced toward her sister.

Brittany lay motionless, her pale face marred by the gash near her temple and other bruises turning purple across her forehead, cheeks and chin.

When Jenna turned back to Cliff, he had pulled his T-shirt back over his head and was tucking it into his waistband.

"Why a frog skeleton tattoo? Why not the whole frog?" she asked.

His gaze slid away as he pushed his arms into the sleeves of his black leather jacket. "It's in honor of a deployment where one of our own gave the ultimate sacrifice." He tipped his head toward Brittany. "Is she going to be all right? She's pretty banged up."

"I think so," Jenna said. "She's tougher than she looks."

One corner of his mouth lifted. "Like her sister?"

Though Jenna's training had been hard, her sister's life choices had been harder. "Even more so. She could use a break."

Brittany's passionate desire to keep her baby girl was a complete turnaround from the young woman who had never seemed to have a direction and never settled for long in one place.

"I have to find her baby," Jenna whispered. "She needs her mother." The truth was, they needed each other.

"Your sister said the kidnapper attacked her," Cliff said quietly. "Do you think it was the baby's daddy?"

Jenna shrugged. "Maybe. He's definitely a person of interest. As is the man who wanted to adopt her baby. I want to interview each of them. I also need to spend some time on my office computer. I just don't feel like I can leave Brittany right now."

"You know, Hank Patterson's computer guy is supposed to be good at finding information about people and organizations. I can feed him the names you have and let him get started."

Her lips twisted for a moment. "I don't think I want to know where his guy gets his information. I have access to a number of criminal databases. But I'm thinking more is better when it comes to finding the baby." She nodded. "I can give him the names of the two men and the address where Brittany lived with the ex-boyfriend in Billings." She pulled out her cell phone and looked up the Billings address she'd saved when she'd sent Brittany a gift on her birthday.

Jenna and Cliff exchanged phone numbers, and she shared the address with him and the names of the two men.

"I'm sending this information to my new boss,

Stone Jacobs, and to Hank Patterson. Stone's tech support, Kyla Russell, works with Hank's guy. If we have both of them work on this, they might approach it with different perspectives." He nodded toward his phone. "I'm going to give them a heads-up and a quick rundown of what's happened." His eyebrows dipped as he met her gaze. "Are you all right with it? I know law enforcement and the FBI have their own protocols. I don't want to step on anyone's toes."

Jenna snorted. "We're talking about my family. All bets are off. I'll pull out every stop to find that baby. Do it."

He glanced toward her sleeping sister. "I'll conduct the call in the waiting room. It's late, and I don't want to disturb patients."

"I'm staying here," Jenna said. "I don't want the state or local police to come back to question Brittany again. This unit is short-staffed as it is. They can't stand guard over every patient."

Cliff nodded. "I'll be right back." He turned to go.

A pang of guilt tugged at Jenna. "Cranston," she called out.

He turned back to her. "Yes?"

"You don't have to do this," she said. "The fact you ran into me in the stairwell doesn't make you responsible for me or what happens to my family. There are plenty of people working this case, and you're not even a member of law enforcement."

He faced her, holding her gaze. "Your sister was

attacked. Your niece was taken. If I were you, I'd do anything in my power to help my sister and save her niece."

She nodded. Involving a stranger in solving a case went against everything she'd learned in training. "What if working with me on this case puts you in danger?"

His lips turned upward on the corners. "Sweetheart, I was and always will be a Navy SEAL. I've seen some of the worst things a human can do to other humans. Gone up against people who don't value the lives of others, including women and children. I've been shot, hit by shrapnel and lived through a helicopter crash."

"Right." Images of the scars across his back and side flashed through her memory. He'd been in many more dangerous situations than she'd ever imagined. He had the physical scars to prove it. And, based on his admission about having a panic attack when he'd run into the stairwell, he also had mental scars.

He crossed to her and took her hands in his. "Do you want me to back off? Walk away? Leave you and your sister alone?"

She stared up into light blue eyes that seemed to be windows into his soul, and her knees wobbled just a little. "No," she said without consciously conjuring the word.

This man. This stranger had burst into her life,

perhaps at the worst time, but maybe at the time she needed him most.

"I've worked every case of missing persons that has come across my desk as if that person was one of my loved ones," she said, her fingers curling around hers. "But this…"

"Is your sister," he finished softly.

"Up until now, I might not have been the best big sister, but damn." A lump rose in her throat, threatening to cut off her air. She swallowed hard, forcing it back. "Brittany and her baby are my only family." Her grip tightened on his. "I'll do anything to keep them safe."

He bent and pressed his lips to her forehead. "I'll get Stone and Hank working on finding anything relating to the two men and your sister. And I'll let Stone know I won't be starting the new job until we get the baby back."

Jenna's heart pinched hard in her chest. "What if we never find—"

Cliff pressed a calloused finger to her lips, shaking his head. "Not an option. We'll get her back."

Used to working alone, Jenna had to admit it was comforting to know this Navy SEAL was on her team, working toward the same purpose.

She nodded, her spine stiffening and her resolve hardening. This was what she did. She solved cases. She pushed aside the fact that so many missing children were never found. So many cases that were never solved.

Her fists clenched, and her jaw hardened. This was her niece. Her sister's baby. Losing her forever was...

Not a damned option.

CHAPTER 4

CLIFF LEFT Jenna in the hospital room with her sedated sister and walked to the end of the hall, where he'd spied a waiting room near the elevator.

He pushed through the door and noted the vending machines for snacks and coffee, a reminder that he hadn't eaten since breakfast. But he wasn't there for food. He dialed Stone's number.

"Cranston," Stone answered on the first ring. "How's Gus?"

For a split second, Cliff couldn't process Stone's question. He'd almost forgotten why he'd come to the hospital in the first place. "Gus was doing well when I left him a while ago. If he has a good night, they'll release him tomorrow."

"Good. Glad to hear his surgery went well," Stone said. "Will you be heading down to West Yellowstone after you drop him at the Bright Days

Ranch? Or will you be staying a night before coming here?"

"I meant to call you earlier and let you know that the physical therapist from the ranch is headed to Bozeman tomorrow and can pick up Gus and take him back with her."

"Even better," Stone said. "Then you'll be here tomorrow. I'll let the staff know to have a room ready for you at the lodge."

Cliff shook his head even though he knew Stone couldn't see him. "That won't be necessary. At least not yet."

"Are you having second thoughts about coming to work for Brotherhood Protectors?" Stone asked. "I promise we do good things, have a positive purpose and operate as a team. You won't find a job anywhere else that will utilize your combat training and experience for such a good cause."

Cliff chuckled. "You can save the sales pitch. I'm already sold. It's just that I've run into a situation and need to stay here until it's resolved. And I'll need help from yours and Hank's tech gurus."

"Whatcha got?" Stone asked, his tone serious.

Cliff filled him in on what had happened with the attack on Brittany and the stolen baby. He told him about running into FBI Special Agent Jenna Jenkins in the stairwell, omitting the part about the panic attack.

"I want to stick around and help if I can," Cliff

ELLE JAMES

said. "The city and state police are working the case. I doubt they'll ask the FBI to step in unless they have reason to believe the baby has been transported across state lines."

"I would think Jenkins wouldn't be allowed to work the case anyway since it involves her relative," Stone commented. "Of course, you should stay. I'm sure Special Agent Jenkins will be conducting her own unofficial investigation. I would if it involved my sister and her baby."

"She will," Cliff agreed.

"What can we help with?"

"I have the names of two men who are persons of interest and Brittany Berry's address in Billings." Cliff put Stone on speaker and brought up the text message Jenna had sent him. "Forwarding the information now." He sent the data via text. "You said you have a computer guru on staff there in West Yellowstone."

"That would be Kyla. She's so smart, it's almost scary. She finds the information others might miss and can piece things together that don't necessarily appear to relate. The woman is amazing," Stone said. "And she works closely with Hank's guy, Swede. They make a formidable team, working remotely. I can have them run the names."

"Thanks," Cliff said. "As for when I'll report to the new job, I can't give you an exact date."

Stone chuckled. "Your official start date is today."

Cliff frowned. "I'm sorry. Did you hear me when I said I wouldn't be able to report to West Yellowstone for a while?"

"I heard you," Stone said. "As so many of us have done, you've fallen into your first assignment as a Brotherhood Protector."

"I don't understand. No one here has asked to hire us. I'm volunteering my help to Special Agent Jenkins. She's not paying me to be here."

"Right," Stone said. "Hank doesn't always charge for the services we provide. He and Sadie are committed to seeing justice served regardless of a client's ability to pay. They think it's more important to protect, rescue and extract first. If the client can afford to pay, good. If not, Hank and Sadie will make sure you get paid. Money isn't a factor in whether or not we'll take a case."

"Are you serious?" Cliff asked.

Stone laughed. "As a heart attack. Knowing Sadie, Hank's wife, she'd be the first to insist you help get that baby back to its mother. They have two children of their own."

Warmth filled Cliff's chest and spread throughout his body. For the first time since the explosion that had killed his friend and changed his life, he felt a sense of purpose.

Ever since Syria, he'd wondered why Dutton had died, and he'd been spared.

Was this why? Was he meant to leave the Navy

and land in Bozeman with Gus's gallstones and a panic attack that sent him plowing into Jenna Jenkins?

"Anything you need, let us know," Stone continued. "Or go directly to Hank. They're a little closer. If you need weapons, communications devices or backup, all you have to do is call. We're a team and can deploy to any situation on short notice."

A smile playing across his lips, Cliff said, "I believe I've made the right choice."

"And what choice is that?" Stone asked.

"Signing on with Brotherhood Protectors."

Again, Stone laughed. "We've all felt the same. Now, go find that baby. We'll be in contact with any information we can find. And let me tell you, Kyla and Swede can tap into data not all law enforcement agencies can access. If there's info to be found, they'll find it."

"Good to know," Cliff said. "The sooner they can get us a lead, the better."

"And Cliff," Stone went on, "Are you still having nightmares and day terrors?"

Cliff stiffened. "How do you know about that?" His health records were supposed to be private.

Stone sighed. "When I said Swede and Kyla have access to data...well, suffice it to say, I've read your file. PTSD is real. Don't ignore it. Sometimes, talking about what you're feeling can help. If not with a therapist, then with a friend. Someone who has been, and still is, working through his own issues."

"You have flashbacks?" Cliff asked.

"I do," Stone said. "There are nights the dreams make me wake up swinging, or I have to force myself awake to keep from reliving the death of my best friend. We've seen too much. Lived through horrors most folks who've never served will never experience. It leaves wounds that may never heal. Wounds to our souls."

Cliff's chest was so tight he could barely breathe. Stone's words were spot on. "Do the nightmares ever go away?" Cliff asked. Or the day terrors that send him spinning into a panic attack?

"I doubt they'll ever go away," Stone said softly. "They do come less often. Again, if you need someone to talk to, any one of us will listen and do anything we can to help."

"Thanks," Cliff said. "I need to get back to Jenna."

"Right," Stone said. "Out here."

"Out here," Cliff echoed as if they were communicating on radio headsets, not cell phones.

He pressed the button to sever the connection and stared down at the device in his hand.

Gus would be on his way to the Brighter Days Rehab ranch to work on his physical and mental recovery from injuries incurred during that explosion in Syria. Cliff admired the man for his courage to admit he needed help.

Cliff had convinced himself he could power through the panic attacks and heal himself over time. The hours he'd spent with the therapist after they'd redeployed following the Syrian mission had given him some techniques to use when he felt a panic attack coming on. Too often, things happened fast, and he wasn't able to apply those techniques to slow or avoid the outcome.

The psychiatrist had prescribed medicine to help, but Cliff hadn't liked the way it made him feel and had stopped taking it after less than a week.

He hoped he didn't lose his shit to a panic attack while working with the FBI agent. He needed to be operating at one hundred percent to give his best effort to the search and recovery of one newborn infant. He'd promised Jenna they'd bring her niece home. He refused to fail at this mission.

He pocketed his cell phone and pulled his credit card out of his wallet.

His stomach rumbled as he stood in front of the snack machine. Slipping his credit card into the slot, he studied the options. After a moment, he selected a package of powdered donuts, a honeybun and a bag of potato chips and removed his credit card from the reader.

Snacks in hand, he walked quietly down the corridor to the room where Jenna waited with her sister, probably hoping the authorities would get lucky and find the baby before her sister woke.

As an FBI agent, she'd already be making a list of the things she needed to do, the places and people she needed to check.

He tapped lightly on the door before pushing it open enough to duck his head inside.

Jenna Jenkins was halfway out of her chair when she realized it was him. She sank back down, her shoulders relaxing. "How'd your boss take your announcement that you weren't going to start the job for a while?" she asked in a soft tone, just barely above a whisper.

Cliff dropped his purchases on the rolling table. "He told me my start date was today."

Her brow twisted. "Surely, he doesn't expect you to drive to Yellowstone in the middle of the night."

Cliff shook his head. "No. He's already given me my new assignment, and it's here in Bozeman."

"Oh," she said, a frown forming. "Does that mean you're heading out?"

"No," he said, keeping his face devoid of any hint of emotion.

Her frown deepened. "Did you quit?"

He chuckled. "No."

She sighed. "I don't understand."

"You're not getting rid of me anytime soon." His lips turned up in a smile. "My first assignment is to help you find your sister's baby."

"We're your assignment?"

He nodded. "And I sent him the data you gave me.

Kyla and Swede will look for anything they can find on the two men."

Jenna pressed a hand to her chest and closed her eyes for a moment. "Remind me to thank your boss for the assistance."

"Will do." His gaze took in her sleeping sister. "What now?"

"I want so desperately to get to my office and start going through criminal databases. Since I haven't been invited to help the local and state authorities in their interviews, I'll have to think of creative ways to question the people without stepping on local law enforcement's toes or cases."

"Are we going now?" Cliff asked.

"Sadly, no. We have to wait until morning to do anything. Plus, I want to be here when Brittany wakes. There's a possibility they'll send her home tomorrow. I'll need to pack her up and transport her to my house."

"Are you going to sleep?" Cliff asked.

"I'm considering it. Though, I'm not quite sure how to get comfortable in this chair."

He glanced around the room, his gaze landing on the cushioned window seat that provided even more seating for guests. "Why don't you sleep on the window seat? I can sleep in the chair."

Nurse Angie entered the room, carrying a pillow and a stack of blankets. "You two staying here tonight?"

"Perfect." Jenna rose from the chair and reached for the pillow and blankets.

The nurse checked Brittany's vitals again and gently adjusted the pillow behind the patient's head. When she finished, she adjusted the lights to almost dark. "Let me know if you need anything," Angie said and disappeared.

"You can have the window seat," Jenna said.

Cliff shook his head. "I'm too tall. You would be more comfortable there."

She handed him a blanket he was surprised to discover was still warm. He held it against his chest, watching as Jenna crossed to the window and laid the pillow and a blanket on the cushion.

Cliff dropped into the chair Jenna had vacated. It was still warm from her body.

He leaned back, excited that the ugly piece of furniture had a high headrest. As he leaned further back, a footrest rose beneath his calves. The chair was a recliner. Pulling the blanket over his arms and shoulders, he settled in, determined to get some sleep.

Just not yet.

Jenna spread the blanket on the window seat and sat on the edge, kicking off her shoes. She glanced across at him. "Good. I'm glad that you'll be able to stretch out."

"I'm not sure I'd call it stretching out, but it beats a foxhole full of rainwater."

Jenna laid on her side, her head on the pillow, and draped the blanket over her arms and shoulders.

The dim lighting in the room made it hard for Cliff to determine if her eyes were open or closed.

"What about you?" she said softly.

"What about me?"

"Do you have a family?"

He started toward her dark figure, wishing he could see her eyes and read her expression and body language. Whispered words in the darkness seemed ungrounded and impersonal without context.

"No family. My folks were older when they had me. They lived long enough to see me graduate from BUD/S to become a SEAL."

Cliff's father had been so proud. His mother had been, too, but her pride had been tempered. She'd understood the danger he'd face and feared for his life every time he deployed. Sadly, or thankfully, she'd passed before the Syrian mission that had killed others on his team and had so nearly killed him.

"Do you have a wife somewhere? Children?" Jenna asked. "You don't have to answer if I'm getting too personal. I mean, you did kiss my forehead. Although, you could just as easily kiss a child's forehead, and it wouldn't mean anything more than a mild affection." She stopped abruptly. "Sorry. I should let you sleep. We'll be busy in the morning."

He smiled in the darkness. "It's okay. I didn't see the point. No woman should have to put up with the uncertainty of a spouse who's married to the Navy. So many of the women my teammates married ultimately divorced them and found men who didn't deploy at a moment's notice to top-secret locations they weren't allowed to disclose. They chose men who worked nine-to-five jobs and came home to them every night."

"Sad," she said. "But I get it. My father was in the Marine Corps until I was twelve. Up until my father retired, my mother raised Brittany and me. My father was never around. Although, I think it was almost the opposite for my mother. She liked it when he was gone. She had full control of the household. When my father returned, it was always a power play between my mother and father."

"I heard other members of my team talk about similar struggles in their home lives," Cliff said.

"When my step-father retired from active duty, the arguments increased. They managed to stay together until my little sister graduated high school, and I was in my last semester of college. They'd met with an attorney one afternoon to discuss their divorce. On their way home, they were involved in a head-on collision with a drunk driver. Our parents died instantly. The drunk driver walked away with minor injuries."

"I'm sorry about your parents," he said. "I bet it was hard for your sister."

"I don't know. From what my mother told me,

Brittany was tired of taking orders from her Marine Corps father and eager to get out on her own. She knew all the buttons to push to stir our parents up." Jenna snorted softly. "She pushed them often, hung out with the wrong crowd and probably dabbled in drugs. I'm almost certain her teenage shenanigans were the straw that broke the camel's back on our parents' marriage. They were both strong individuals with different ideas on parenting and discipline."

"She was eighteen when they passed?" he asked.

"Yeah. Dad wanted her to join the military and get a little discipline. Mom got her accepted into college here in Bozeman. She moved into my apartment with me the summer after I graduated college. It was rough. I wasn't ready to play mother to a rebellious teen."

"Let me guess," Cliff said. "You were the rule-follower."

She sighed in the dark. "Yeah. It rubbed Brittany wrong in so many ways. I was accepted into the Montana Law Enforcement Academy. I only had time to help her move into her dorm and then left for my twelve-week training program. We weren't allowed much contact with folks back home. In retrospect, I should've delayed my entry to give Brittany time to adjust to college life and the loss of our parents. Although, I'm not sure I'd have been much influence on her choices. She dropped out halfway through the semester and moved with her boyfriend to Seattle. Since then, she's been pretty much on her own, except for the occasional help I've given her when she needed money to start over after a breakup."

Cliff felt a pang of guilt talking about the woman sleeping in the room, who'd just given birth and been brutalized.

"What about you?" he asked, wanting to know more about the older sister. "You went to Montana's police academy. How did you end up in the FBI?"

"It was always my goal to join the FBI. I majored in Criminal Justice with a minor in Forensic Science. The FBI wants applicants to have a degree and a couple of years of experience. While I was in college, I interned with the Bozeman Police Department. It helped me get into the police academy, although they would've taken me without it. I graduated with a 4.0."

"An internship, a major and a minor, *and* you came out with a 4.0 grade-point average?" He shook his head. "I'm impressed."

"That's what happens when you don't have much of a social life. I had a plan. I didn't deviate from that plan."

"No frat parties? Dating?" He couldn't imagine a woman as attractive as Jenna going through college without a date.

"I had a couple of study dates with guys from some of my classes, but they weren't as serious about learning the test information as I was. They were more into making out. They didn't call for a second date. I was glad. Besides, I wasn't very...experienced."

"Didn't you date in high school?"

"A couple of times. More to make my mom happy than because I wanted to. I had a gay boyfriend."

"What?" Cliff lifted his head, wishing he could see her face as she spoke of her past.

Jenna chuckled. "We were both in the gifted and talented program. My mother wanted me to date and get some experience with boys before I went to college. Brent hadn't come out because he didn't want to be bullied through high school."

Cliff remembered pulling a couple of jocks off a guy who'd dared to wear a rainbow-colored T-shirt to high school in honor of gay-pride week. "Teens can be cruel," he commented.

"Exactly," Jenna agreed. "We were juniors, both being pressured by our parents to go to Junior-Senior Prom, neither wanting the hassle or the drama of finding a date. Our parents insisted we go as a rite of passage, a chance to make memories of our days in high school."

Images of his own prom filled Cliff's memories. He'd asked one of the cheerleaders. She'd turned him down and accepted an offer from a buff football player. He'd been in track and on the swim team, but that wasn't as cool. After being rejected and his ego having taken a hit, he couldn't bring himself to ask another cheerleader, only to be similarly refused.

He'd asked the girl who'd always sat alone at lunch, reading a book. He could still picture her in her thick-framed glasses, jeans and a baggy T-shirt, startled that someone was addressing her. When he'd asked her to prom, she'd been so flustered she'd spilled her drink on her book. Despite the accident, she'd accepted his invitation.

For a night that he'd had such low expectations for, it had turned out to be one he'd remember with a grin for the rest of his life. When he'd gone to Alyssa's house to pick her up, she'd transformed from the bookworm into a beautiful young woman in a black dress with crystal embellishments that sparkled when the light caught them. She'd traded her glasses for contacts and had her hair piled high, exposing a long, slender neck. The dress accentuated the curves hidden beneath the baggy shirts and blue jeans.

They'd had fun, dancing the night away. Though their relationship hadn't grown into anything more intimate, they'd ended up being good friends and still kept in touch with at least a card at Christmas.

"My problem," Jenna continued her story, "was that no one asked me to go to the prom. I had no desire to go alone, and I didn't have a posse of girlfriends to go with me. Brent didn't want to go with a girl and have her think he was interested. We stayed after school for the debate club and were the last ones out of the room. I asked him how I could get a guy to ask me to a prom I had no desire to attend just to make my mother happy. He laughed and said he wished he knew the answer to that and that he wanted to go, but not with a girl. I don't think he meant to let it slip. I promised I wouldn't out him. He was worried that if I knew he was gay, others would know as well. That's when we made a pact to be a couple until we graduated high school and left the small town and small minds behind."

Cliff grinned. "Brilliant."

"We had a date for prom, he helped me find a dress and even taught me how to do a few dance moves so that I didn't look like a complete loser on the dance floor. For the rest of our junior and senior years, we went out on dates, dutch, of course, and held hands in the hallways. No one bothered us or questioned the authenticity of our relationship. It helped that we were fairly invisible to the popular groups. Bottom line...we survived high school. Brent moved to Seattle, where he met and married a philosophy student. He's happy, his parents weren't surprised when he came out, saying they'd known since he was in grade school. Dating me had confused them, but they understood his reasons."

"You didn't meet anyone in college or on the job?" he asked.

A long silence stretched between them.

He didn't say anything but found himself holding his breath. By her sudden silence, he suspected there had been someone and might still be.

Her tone lowering, she finally said, "Not so much in college. It wasn't until I joined the FBI. At the academy, trainees don't have time to eat or breathe. After I completed my training, I was assigned to an office in Virginia, where I met a guy who lived in the apartment next to mine. With training behind me, I had a little downtime and took up bicycling. He was an avid cycler. We struck up a conversation that lasted into the evening and dinner. We lived together for five years."

"Still married to him?" Cliff asked, his chest tight.

She snorted. "We never married. And no. We're not together anymore."

"What happened?"

"Nothing," she answered, her tone flat. "He never asked me to marry him. One day, he said it wasn't working. The next day, he moved out, and I transferred to Bozeman."

Cliff winced. "Ouch."

"Him leaving wasn't what hurt," she said, her voice tight.

"What did?"

"Three months after he left, he married his secretary, and now, he has a kid on the way."

"If it didn't hurt when he left, why did it hurt when he married and had a kid?"

"I don't know," she said. "I guess because it hurt my pride. We lived together for five years. He never once hinted at marriage and children. As soon as he left me, he had both."

He hadn't known Jenna long, but something about her drew him to her and made him want to know her better and shield her from pain. Cliff wasn't sure he wanted to know the answer, but he asked anyway, "Did you love him?"

"No," she said softly. "I thought I did. But then, my parents didn't set the best example. I'm not sure if I'd recognize love if it hit me in the face."

"Do you miss him?" Cliff asked.

"No," Jenna said. "For a while, I missed knowing there was someone to come home to. But I realized I could have that same feeling if I got a dog. So, I did." She gave a short laugh. "Brutus is great company. He's not mad when I'm late, is happy to see me every time I walk through the door and loves me unconditionally, just as I love him. Like when you were in the Navy, your job kept you away. My job isn't forty hours a week. I'm on call 24/7. Relationships are work and require time and effort. I don't have time to give the effort."

Cliff had no idea why he was talking about love to a woman he'd just met, but he couldn't stop. "Have you ever considered you haven't met that person who makes you *want* to take the time…to make the effort?"

"No," she said without hesitation.

"You've never been in love, have you?" he asked into the night.

For a long moment, silence reigned.

"I love my dog," she offered. "He doesn't judge me."

"You've never felt passion so profound you feel like you could spontaneously combust with the amount of joy expanding inside you?" he persisted.

She chuckled. "No. Why would I want to spontaneously combust? Think of the mess I'd leave behind for someone else to clean. And if you're talking about having an orgasm, I don't need someone else to give that to me. I have BOB."

A stab of something resembling jealousy hit him square in the gut. "Who's Bob?"

Another chuckle warmed the air in the room. "Battery. Operated. Boyfriend. Where have you been?"

"Fighting wars," he answered, grinning at the thought of her using a sex toy to get off. It was funny and kind of sad. Apparently, she hadn't been in love and hadn't had mind-blowing sex.

He wanted to yell, *challenge accepted,* but had the sense to know she wouldn't appreciate it and would likely throw up a wall of resistance if she had a clue that a man was willing to push past her don't-fuck-with-me, hard-core exterior to the soft, squishy, tenderhearted, dog-loving woman beneath. Anyone who wanted to get past her defenses wouldn't accomplish that goal with a full-frontal attack. He'd have to be more subtle.

"You're right," she said. "I haven't met someone who makes me want to spend more time with him or someone who can do a better job than BOB. I don't believe he exists."

He murmured softly, "Until you met me."

CHAPTER 5

JENNA LAY on her side on the window seat, facing her sister's bed. She could make out her sister's form beneath the white sheets and blanket. Beyond her, the Navy SEAL half-lounged in the chair on the other side of Brittany's bed.

She could only see the silhouette of his head and the dark smudge of his black hair. She couldn't tell if his eyes were opened or closed.

The darkness hid their expressions from each other, making her feel less inhibited. Why else would she have given him her life story? She'd probably bored him to death, or worse, made him pity her pathetic love life.

She hadn't opened up to anyone, not even Brittany, about her past or the bargain she'd made with Brent to be her gay boyfriend in high school. If she had hoped to impress him with her strength and courage, her admission to dating a gay guy was a one-way train ride to her own pity party. Or more like a train wreck.

Not that she should care what Cliff Cranston thought of her. They barely knew each other. As soon as they found Baby Blakely, Cliff would leave for his next assignment with the Brotherhood Protectors. She'd never see him again.

Jenna strained to hear the sound of movement inside the room and in the hallway on the other side of the door.

She wasn't sure why she'd allowed Cliff to hang around as long as he had. Then again, any help she could get to find the baby was appreciated.

But that wasn't the only reason. Something about the man had captivated her and made her want to get to know him. And the more she learned, the more she wanted to know.

Like what had he experienced that was so traumatic it had left a mark on his psyche and cursed him with panic attacks so intense, he felt the need to run into stairwells? Had he run into the stairwell to get away from the demons plaguing him or because he was embarrassed by his inability to control himself?

She couldn't deny that the tattoo of the bone frog had touched her. Too often, guys got tattoos in honor of their current lady love or their favorite motorcycle. Honoring a fallen comrade was touching and made her heart hurt for his loss. However, the other scars marring his skin were more disturbing. Were they battle scars?

Jenna had fought the urge to reach out and trace them with her fingertips. What did they feel like? How hard were those muscles in his arms and shoulders that rippled with every move? And how the hell did he maintain washboard abs? He wasn't a young man in his twenties. Taut muscles like his were the product of discipline and self-control.

She worked out every day, if possible. As an FBI agent, she was expected to stay fit.

She sighed. Sleep was elusive. When she wasn't thinking about Cliff, her mind churned with what little they knew so far and how they'd obtain more information and clues as to who'd stolen the baby.

She must have fallen asleep. A noise jerked her awake. The large swinging door opened, and a woman entered carrying an organizer full of glass tubes. She adjusted the lighting, making it brighter.

Jenna rolled off the window seat and rubbed the sleep from her eyes long enough to check the woman's badge. The face in the picture matched the woman.

'I'm here to draw blood," she whispered.

"Do you have to wake her?" Jenna asked.

The woman grimaced. "I try to be gentle, but the process usually wakes the patient anyway."

"It's okay," Brittany whispered. "I'm awake, for now."

ELLE JAMES

While the technician drew a vial of blood, Nurse Smalls breezed in on silent feet and checked Brittany's vital signs. "Looking good," she said softly. "The doctor will probably release you tomorrow so you can go home to recuperate."

"Without my baby," Brittany said, her tone flat. She pressed a hand to her chest and glanced toward Jenna hopefully.

Every time her sister looked at her like that, it was as if a giant hand gripped Jenna's heart and squeezed the life out of it. "Sorry," she said. "We haven't heard anything."

Brittany drew in a ragged breath and let it out slowly.

Nurse Smalls handed her a cup filled with ice water. "Drink as much as you can. You'll want to make sure your kidneys are functioning. You'll have to pee before you're released."

Brittany fitted the straw in her mouth and drank as much as she could. When she'd had enough, she held out the cup.

Jenna took it and set it on the nightstand. "It's only four-thirty. You might as well go back to sleep again."

"That's right," Nurse Smalls said. "The doctor won't be in until around eight o'clock."

Brittany nodded. "Might as well. No reason to be awake when all I can do is worry." She shook her head. "I feel so helpless. I should be out there looking for her."

"No," Jenna said. "You've just given birth. You need to give yourself time to recover. The police are working the case. They promised to keep me informed if they find anything."

Brittany nodded and held out her hand.

Jenna took it and squeezed gently. "We'll find her."

"Thank you for being here for me," Brittany whispered. "For both of us."

Jenna's gut churned. This was her little sister. She'd always helped her when she was in a bad situation. She couldn't let her down now. "I love you, Brit. We'll find her," she repeated.

Her sister's eyes fluttered closed.

Jenna held her hand until it went limp, then tucked it beneath the blanket.

With any chance of going back to sleep nil, she quietly paced the length of the room, going over everything Brittany had told her about the attack, her boyfriend and the man who'd supported her for the last couple of weeks of her pregnancy for the right to adopt her baby.

She needed to get out and question these people.

Brittany had walked out on Larry Sutton. Was he angry that she'd left him? Would he steal the baby to get his revenge? If so, what would he do with the baby? If he was married with children of his own, he couldn't just take the infant home and add her to his family without some explanation.

"I'd tell you that pacing isn't going to solve anything, but I know better. I do some of my best problem-solving when I'm pacing, walking or jogging," Cliff said softly.

"I keep thinking that we have two persons of interest. What if neither one of them had anything to do with the abduction? We might have an unsub with his own motivation for taking the baby."

"True." Cliff pushed to his feet and stretched his arms high above his head. "The ex-boyfriend was the father. Motivation enough to take the baby if he wanted the child and didn't want your sister to raise her." He lowered his arms and twisted side to side. "The man who supported your sister with the intention of adopting her baby might've suspected she would renege on their bargain and took matters into his own hands."

"They're too obvious," she said.

Cliff stopped in front of her. "Maybe so."

"But we have to chase every lead until we find her." Jenna pinched the bridge of her nose, squeezing gritty, sleep-deprived eyes closed for a moment. "I just need to get out there and start looking."

"Do you have a friend or neighbor who could stay with your sister while you work?" he asked.

Her brow furrowed. "Mrs. McAnally, my sixty-seven-year-old neighbor, takes care of my dog when

I'm working late. She's a retired nurse. I might get her to help." Jenna pulled her cell phone out of her pocket and started to dial.

Cliff covered her hand with his. "You might wait until seven or eight o'clock. It's not even five yet."

Her hand tingled where he'd touched hers. "Right," she said and quickly withdrew her hand, shoving it and the cell phone into her pocket. Though he was no longer touching her, the tingling continued, a warmth spreading from her hand through her body.

Jenna stepped away and resumed her pacing. "I hate that we have to wait to do anything. The seconds are ticking away. Whoever stole the baby could be taking her further and further away with each passing minute. If I had my laptop, I might be able to do some digging."

"I could stay with Brittany if you want to go home to get it," Cliff offered.

Her brow furrowed. "I barely know you…"

"But somewhere, deep inside, you trust me." He smiled. "You can't help it. And that—"

"—bugs the crap out of me," she finished and sighed. "And reassures me at the same time. Okay, I'll run home for my laptop and be right back. I don't want to miss the doctor if he comes early."

"Are you sure you'll be all right going home alone at this time?" Cliff asked.

Her lips twisted. "I do it all the time."

"Right." He held out his hand. "Let me have your phone."

She reached into her pocket, frowning. "I might need it."

"I only want it for a minute." He took the phone from her hand, glanced at the screen and handed it back. "Unlock it, please."

She did as he said and handed it back.

Cliff added a phone number with his name on it to her contacts list. After he called himself from her phone, he handed it back. "Now, you have my number. If you run into trouble, call me. If it's bad trouble, call 911 first, then call me."

She slid the phone back into her pocket, the device still warm from his hands. "It goes both ways. If anything happens here..."

"I'll call immediately." He walked with her to the door. "Don't worry about us. I'll be with Brittany the entire time. Go." For the second time since she'd met him, he bent and brushed his lips across her forehead.

She raised a hand to the spot, heat filling her cheeks. "Why do you keep doing that?"

He shrugged. "I don't know. It just feels natural."

"Do you do that with all the girls?"

"Not actually. There's something about your forehead that begs to be kissed." He turned her around and gave her a gentle push. "You don't want to miss the doctor, and your sister will want to see you when she wakes. Don't be long."

"Yes, sir," she said and popped a salute. "And thanks." She hurried out to the elevator and took it to the ground floor. The circus of police had long since gone, along with the people they'd detained. The only people in the hospital entrance were a couple of security guards and two Bozeman police officers, apparently providing additional backup.

Jenna made it a point to check in with them and let them know who she was and that she'd be back in less than thirty minutes to stay with her sister.

She left the hospital and made her way to the car she'd parked the evening before when her sister had begged her to come to the hospital. She hadn't known then why her sister was there or that she'd given birth to a baby girl.

The hours that had passed seemed like a lifetime. She'd gone from having one family member to two and back to one in the few short hours. And now, she was running an investigation on the sidelines to find her newest family member.

Add a handsome, tattooed and scarred Navy SEAL she couldn't get rid of, and her life had gone from ordered and simple to what-the-fuck crazy.

"Wow," she murmured as she slipped behind the wheel of her candy-apple red Jeep Wrangler and started the engine. As she pulled out of her parking space, she circled around the hospital, looking for the different exit doors, places a person could hide and anything that might help her understand how someone could walk into a hospital and steal a baby. She slowed as she passed the loading dock.

At the very least, the police ought to have located the truck by now. It couldn't be easy to hide something that big. And once they found it, hopefully, they could lift prints that would identify the person who'd driven it.

As much as she'd like to spend more time examining the loading dock and the corridors and rooms leading to it, she needed to retrieve her laptop and get back to Brittany before she woke again. The sleeping medication they'd given her would be wearing off, and Brittany would be alert enough to make herself sick with worry.

The drive to her little cottage on the northeast corner of town didn't take long that early in the morning. Most people were in bed, getting those last few minutes of sleep before their alarm clocks went off and they had to get ready for work or school.

The routine of their lives seemed so repetitive and calm compared to Jenna's.

As she pulled into the driveway of her small white clapboard house, she smiled at the light shining over the front porch.

She didn't have to ask Mrs. McAnally to check on her dog. The woman loved looking out her front picture windows at the other houses in the neighborhood. She was always the first to notice and report on anything out of the ordinary. Less than a week after Jenna had moved in, Mrs. McAnally had marched over to welcome her, carrying a fragrant loaf of banana nut bread.

The older woman knew that if Jenna's red Jeep wasn't parked in the driveway by seven in the evening, Brutus would need to go out and be fed. And she always turned on the light over the porch so that Jenna didn't have to fumble for her house key in the dark.

Brutus had loved the older woman from the start when she'd patted his head and told him he was a good boy. The German shepherd acted starved for attention and soaked up all the affection anyone wanted to give.

Mrs. McAnally had gone one step further by giving him a special treat, a tasty strip of chicken jerky. Since that first meeting, she brought him a doggy treat every time. Every time Jenna's neighbor came through the cottage door, Brutus greeted her like a long-lost friend, completely beside himself, his tail wagging so hard it made his entire body wiggle.

Jenna parked in the driveway and got her key out of her pocket before exiting the SUV.

Before she stuck her key in the lock, Brutus barked and scratched at the door, wildly anxious to get to her.

When the door finally swung open, Jenna braced

herself for eighty pounds of German Shepherd exuberant love.

On cue, Brutus launched himself at her.

Jenna dropped to her knees to keep from being knocked off her feet. She wrapped her arms around the dog and hugged him close, tears welling in her eyes. "Oh, Brutus, we have a new member of the family. You're going to love her." She hugged him around the neck and pushed to her feet. "But first, we have to find her and bring her home."

The dog tried to push past her to get outside.

She grabbed his collar and held him while she closed the door. "You can go outside in the backyard," she said, leading him to the back of the house.

As soon as she opened the door, he shot out, barking frantically.

Jenna grabbed the flashlight she kept hanging next to the door and shined it into the yard where Brutus was running along the wooden fence.

"Brutus," she called out. "No barks." Her closest neighbor, Mrs. McAnally, lived alone and shared with Jenna that she slept with an air purifier running for the white noise. Still, Brutus's bark was loud. "Brutus, come," she commanded.

The dog barked several more times as he ran back to where Jenna stood in the doorway.

She bent to smooth a hand over his back. "Did you see a squirrel, boy?"

The shepherd whined softly, the hairs along his

back standing at attention.

"Or was it a cat?" Jenna shined the light again, but all she could see was the weathered wooden fence, not what was on the other side. A wild animal might have wandered into the neighborhood. It happened. An occasional moose or mountain lion wandered through the city.

"Come on," she said, pulling the dog back into the house.

Her laptop was in the living room where she'd left it the day before. She grabbed the device and its charging cords and shoved them into a backpack. When she had what she'd come for, she made a quick pass through the house with an eye for what needed to change to welcome Blakely into her cottage.

The spare bedrooms would have to be emptied, cleaned and furnished with a crib in one room and a full-sized bed in the other. Her desk would have to come out into the living room. She could add a fresh coat of paint to brighten the walls. Space would be tight, but Brittney and the baby would have a roof over their heads and food on the table.

Jenna wanted to be excited about the two of them moving in with her but couldn't see celebrating until Baby Blakely was returned to her mother.

On her way past her room, she stepped in and retrieved her Glock from the nightstand where she'd placed it the night before, not thinking she'd need it to visit her sister in the hospital. After checking that she had a full magazine, she shrugged off her jacket and strapped on her shoulder holster, tucking the weapon inside. Then she pulled on her jacket and left her room.

Jenna checked Brutus's food and water. Mrs. McAnally had refreshed both.

"Sorry, Brutus, but I've got to go," she said as she scratched behind the dog's ear. "If all goes well, I'll be back later today to bring your favorite Aunt."

Brutus stared up at her as he sat in front of the door, his tail wagging hopefully, his muscles tense, ready to spring into action if she said the word for him to come with her.

She flung the strap of the backpack over her shoulder and bent to scratch the dog behind the ear. "I'll be back." Jenna straightened and left the house, locking the door behind her. How many times had she left doors unlocked?

More times than she could count.

Well. Not anymore. When Brittany and the baby moved in, Jenna wouldn't be the only person in the house.

Jenna glanced over her shoulder as she backed out of her driveway. With all her concentration on the rear of her vehicle, she didn't see what slammed into her front windshield until it bounced on the seat beside her, coming to rest on the backpack she'd jammed full of the items she'd returned home to collect.

Adrenaline spiking, Jenna slammed on the brakes, shifted into park and looked around for the person who'd thrown the burnt-orange brick at her vehicle.

Nothing moved, and the shadows were darker than she remembered and sinister.

Based on where the brick had hit her windshield, it had to have come from close to the south corner of her cottage, shrouded in the low-hanging branches of the giant blue spruce she needed to have trimmed or cut down.

She reached beneath her jacket, her hand closing around the pistol grip. Raising the weapon, her thumb hovered over the safety as she studied the shadows beneath the trees. The passenger side of the windshield was shattered with a huge hole through it where the brick had crashed through it.

Had the brick hit the driver's side, it would have landed on Jenna's head.

Heart pounding, Jenna made a conscious decision to remain in her car. Leaving the relative safety of the Jeep exposed her to further flying bricks. She might not be so lucky the next time.

Jenna dug through her back pocket for the detective's business card. It was close to six o'clock. Surely, he'd be awake, getting ready for work. Up or not, he needed to know what had just happened. If the flying brick was in any way related to the attack on her sister—and Jenna suspected it was—the detective needed to know.

Detective Schwope answered on the second ring. "Detective Schwope."

"Sir, this is Special Agent Jenkins. I hate to bother you so early, but I needed to report an incident that might relate to the missing baby case." She told him about returning to her house for her laptop and having a brick fly through her window. "I'd get out and look through the bushes myself, but I don't have backup. As it is, I want to get back to my sister before her doctor does his rounds."

"I'll send a couple of officers to look around," Schwope said.

"Thanks."

"By the way, I'm glad you called. I just got word from dispatch that uniforms found the truck."

"Where was it?" Jenna demanded.

"Parked behind a distribution warehouse on the west end of Bozeman," the detective said. "The back door was open, and the laundry cart was flung onto the ground. Everything in the back was dumped, flung and turned over as if someone was looking for something or very angry. Maybe both."

"Why would the abductor turn the contents of the truck upside down?" Jenna asked.

"Maybe he lost the baby in all the sheets? We don't know. They dusted for prints. No hits yet, but we'll keep you posted."

"Thank you. I'm headed back to the hospital if you need me. The brick will be in my vehicle if you want to send someone to collect it and place it in evidence."

"Will do," the detective said.

Jenna ended the call and drew in a deep breath, letting it out slowly while willing her pulse to slow.

"What the ever-lovin' hell?" she said aloud.

First, her sister had been attacked and her baby taken. Now, Jenna had been targeted as well. Was this more than a play for the baby? Was Larry getting back at Brittany for leaving him by threatening the people she loved?

Or was the wealthy Mr. Waters orchestrating this chaos to make it look like someone else was guilty of taking the baby and terrorizing Brittany and Jenna?

What if they were missing the guilty party altogether?

With her passenger side windshield shattered with a gaping hole through it, a sinister brick as her front passenger seat, Jenna drove across town to the hospital and parked. The gray light of dawn crept into the darkness, giving shape and definition to the fuzzy shadows.

Soon, Jenna would be able to do her own interviewing and information gathering. Hopefully, the Brotherhood Protectors computer techs would find something as well.

After a long night of inaction, Jenna was ready to attack this case and bring her baby niece home.

She prayed they weren't too late.

CHAPTER 6

THE MOMENT JENNA had left the hospital, Cliff had taken her place, pacing the length of the room. He'd been with Jenna since he'd run into her in the stairwell. With her gone, he couldn't shake the feeling of impending doom.

Several times, he'd reached for his cell phone to call her and stopped. She hadn't even been gone thirty minutes. He didn't need to worry until she'd been gone more than an hour, right?

He was on his twentieth pass across the room when his cell phone rang. He glanced at the screen. Hank Patterson's name came up.

His pulse speeding up a notch, Cliff answered the call. "Cranston here," he said.

"Hey, Cliff, how's the young mother holding up?"

Cliff glanced at a sleeping Brittany. Her eyes were closed, but her body moved beneath the sheets, and her head rolled side to side on the pillow, as if she was ducking blows. His heart hurt for the woman who'd just given birth and then had been brutally attacked. "Resting as well as can be expected," he finally answered.

"I'm sure she's distraught over losing her baby," Hank commented. "And the sister, the FBI agent?"

"She made a run to her house for her laptop and left me to watch over Brittany." Cliff glanced at his watch. She'd been gone thirty-five minutes. His hand tightened on the phone he held.

"Have you heard anything from the detectives working the investigation?" Hank asked.

"Nothing so far. Special Agent Jenkins and I plan on asking some of our own questions as soon as we get her sister settled with her neighbor to watch her." He looked at the woman, sleeping fitfully, the bruises getting more colorful than they'd been the night before. "Although, I'm not sure the neighbor will be enough."

"Do I need to send someone over to keep her sister safe while you and the Special Agent work on finding the baby?"

Cliff didn't like making decisions about Brittany and Jenna without running it by them first, but better safe than sorry. "That sounds like a good plan."

"I'll see what I can do. If the stars align, I could have someone there within the next hour."

"Great. Have him check in with me when he gets

to the hospital. The nurse expects the doctor will release Brittany today to recuperate at home."

"I'll keep that in mind. Swede and Kyla have been up all night, combing the internet, looking for anything on Sutton and Waters. They should have a report to you soon."

"Thanks," Cliff said, just beginning to understand why Hank's business was growing so fast. The man cared about the people they were protecting. Hank took a personal interest in the cases and used all his assets to the best of their abilities to make things happen.

"Glad you joined us," Hank said.

"Me, too," Cliff responded. The Brotherhood Protectors might just be the team—no, the family— he hadn't known he needed when he'd left the military.

As soon as he ended his conversation with Hank, Cliff brought up Jenna's number and called it. She answered on the first ring.

"I've only been gone thirty-five minutes," she said. "Miss me already?"

He smiled. The sound of her voice slowed his heartbeat back to a more normal pace. "As a matter of fact, yes. I missed you."

"All is well with Brittany?" she asked.

His gaze went back to Jenna's sister. She was still thrashing and emitted a low moan.

"I think she's having a nightmare." He crossed to stand beside her bed. "Do you want me to wake her?"

"No, I will when I get there," Jenna said, the voice in his receiver echoing in the room. "I'm here."

Cliff spun toward the door to find Jenna standing there, pulling her cell phone away from her ear, a backpack slung over her shoulder.

"You could've told me you were in the building," he said, only mildly irritated that she'd startled him. He was happier to see her than he would have thought he could be, having known her for such a short amount of time.

Brittany moaned again and flung an arm over her face as if shielding herself from imaginary blows.

Jenna was at Cliff's side in seconds, dropping the backpack in a chair.

As she leaned over her sister's bed, something in her hair glistened in the light shining down on her head.

Cliff reached out to capture the shiny object and plucked it from her hair. When he'd first spotted it, he'd thought it was glitter. Once he had it pressed between his thumb and forefinger, he realized it was a much harder material and clear. "This is glass," he said.

Jenna's lips twisted. "Yeah. About that. I'm the proud recipient of a red brick."

Cliff shook his head. "You'll have to give me more

of a clue than that to figure out what the hell you're talking about."

"I was backing out of my driveway when a brick blasted through my windshield and landed in the passenger seat." Jenna reached out and shook her sister gently. "Brittany, wake up, sweetie."

Her sister moaned and pushed Jenna's hand away.

"Wake up, Brittany," Jenna called out softly. "You're having a bad dream. The only way to escape is to wake up. Come on, sweetie, you can do it."

"What do you mean, you're the recipient of a brick?" Cliff touched her arm, forcing her to look his way.

Her mouth tightened. "Someone threw a brick at my car. It crashed through the windshield and landed in the passenger seat."

"What?" Brittany said, her voice little more than a croak. "What happened?"

"Nothing for you to worry about," Jenna reassured her sister.

Brittany's eyes opened, and she squinted up at her sister. "Someone threw a brick at your car?"

Jenna gave her sister a tight smile. "I'm fine. Not hurt."

"But someone threw a brick at your car." Brittany's brow dipped low. "Why? You didn't do anything."

"I don't know." Jenna stroked her sister's arm. "What I do know is that I'm here with you. Relax."

Her sister looked up at Jenna, her worried gaze hopeful. "Have you—"

"—found Baby Blakely?" Jenna shook her head. "Not yet. But we will."

"I should've filled out her name on her birth certificate already," Brittany said. "She deserves an official name."

"You'll have that opportunity when we bring her back to you," Jenna assured her, straightening the sheets around her sister. "You should concentrate on your own recovery. You'll need all your strength and stamina when she's home and keeping you up all night with feedings and diaper changes. Babies are a lot of work."

Brittany nodded. "That's what Larry said when he tried to convince me to give her up for adoption. He said he knew an agency that specialized in placing babies in good homes. He could do all the ground-work." She snorted. "All I had to do was deliver a healthy baby. He'd do the rest. He didn't give a rat's ass about her, or me, for that matter. And the thing is, I feel sorry for his wife and children. That man's fooling around on her, and she doesn't know."

A soft knock sounded on the door, and Nurse Smalls poked her head in. "Oh, good, you're awake." She backed in, carrying a tray. "Thought you might be hungry since you didn't eat last night." She laid the tray on the rolling table and pushed it toward the bed.

Cliff and Jenna stepped back.

The nurse raised the head of the bed so that Brittany was sitting up and moved the table into position over her lap. "There." She walked around the bed to check the IV. "What's your pain level this morning?"

Brittany frowned. "Maybe a four. Mostly sore." She touched the bruise next to her eye and winced.

"That's to be expected. Do you need anything for the pain?" Nurse Smalls asked.

Brittany shook her head. "No. I don't like how groggy it makes me. I can handle it for now."

"Don't think you have to be a hero," the nurse said with a smile. "At the very least, you might consider a mild pain reliever like one you'd take for a headache."

"I'll keep that in mind," Brittany said.

"Then I'll get out of your hair while you eat." She turned to Jenna and Cliff. "The hospital cafeteria is pretty good if you'd like to grab a bite."

"Not for me," Jenna said.

"I'm good," Cliff seconded. He was hungry but wouldn't leave Jenna and Brittany for too long. "I could use a cup of coffee. Where can I get a good cup of coffee on this floor?"

Nurse Smalls smiled. "Skip the vending machine. We have a coffeemaker in the waiting room near the elevator. I just made a fresh pot. I'd bring you some, but I have more patients to feed first." She left the room with a smile.

Cliff met Jenna's gaze. "I'm going for a cup. You want one?"

Jenna nodded. "I'd love one."

"I'll be right back." He left the room, glad to stretch his legs longer than the small room allowed. His long strides ate up the distance between the room and the coffee machine in the waiting room. He poured two cups of coffee, grabbed several packets of sugar and some cream and headed back to Jenna.

Jenna sat beside Brittany's bed while her sister picked at the food on her tray.

"I left all my stuff in the apartment over the bar," Brittany was saying.

Cliff handed the extra coffee cup to Jenna. "Didn't know how you take it, so I got a little of everything." He dropped the packets of sugar and cream on the nightstand beside her.

Jenna smiled up at him. "Thanks. I can drink it black, but I do like a little sugar and cream to cut the bitterness."

"Same," he said and set his cup on the nightstand, tore open a sugar pack and dumped it into his cup, adding a packet of creamer next.

He watched as Jenna added two sugar packets and a creamer to hers, stirred and turned her attention back to Brittany. "Did you want some?"

Brittany's nose wrinkled. "No thanks. I never developed a taste for coffee."

Jenna took a sip, closed her eyes and sighed. "It's my lifeblood. I never would've made it through the academy without it." She opened her eyes and focused on her sister. "I can swing by your apartment today, pack your stuff and move it to my house. I'll need your keys."

"They should be in my purse." Brittany frowned. "They had me put all my clothes and belongings into a plastic bag when I came in. I'm not sure, but I think they stored it all in the closet." She waved her fork toward the closet on the other side of the hospital room.

Jenna took another sip of her coffee, set it down on the nightstand and rose to check in the closet. She pulled out a white plastic bag and riffled through it until she found a small purse and brought it to her sister.

Brittany pushed the table away and emptied the purse on the bed. Several wads of dollar bills, a wallet, a handful of change and a photograph fell onto the sheet. She plucked the wallet out of the middle, opened a zippered compartment and pulled out a single key. She handed the key to Jenna. "The lock can be a little tricky. You have to pull the handle toward you as you turn the key."

Jenna took the key. "You don't keep it on a key ring with your car keys?"

Brittany shook her head. "It's the only key I have. Why bother with a key ring?"

"Where's your car?" Jenna asked.

Brittany looked away. "I sold it a couple of months ago."

Jenna frowned. "Why?"

"We—I needed money for groceries."

"Larry didn't buy groceries?" Jenna shook her head.

"He was paying the rent. I was responsible for groceries. The place where I was working let me go because I was late too many days to work. Morning sickness sucked."

"Dear, sweet Jesus," Jenna murmured.

"You're going to say, *Why didn't you call?*" Brittany's eyes filled. "I couldn't. If I did, it would be the biggest bail-out I ever asked for from you. I was sure once I had the baby, Larry would step up to the plate, our relationship would improve and he'd help out." She shoved her things back into the purse until she came to the photograph. "The bastard never planned to help. I was just a convenient lover who lived in his apartment, kept it clean and was there whenever he came to Billings. I was never going to be anything else to him." She tore the photo in half and flung it aside.

Cliff bent to pick up the pieces and fit them together. "This is Larry?"

She nodded. "That's the bastard."

Cliff tucked the pieces of the photo into his pocket.

Brittany touched her sister's arm. "I'm sorry about your car. I shouldn't have come home to Bozeman and involved you in my drama."

Jenna leaned over to hug her sister. "Shut up."

"No, really," her sister said, her voice trembling. She pushed Jenna away. "If I'd stayed with Larry until the baby was born, I'd have had her in the Billing's hospital, miles away from the janitor who stole my baby."

Cliff hated to agree with Brittany.

Jenna held her sister's hand. "We don't know who took your baby," she argued. "And hindsight won't help. We have to play the cards we've been dealt, and right now, we're doing the best we can."

"When I'm back on my feet," Brittany said, "I'll pay you back for everything I ever took from you—and for the damage to your car."

"Sweetheart," Jenna sank onto the edge of the chair beside Brittany's bed, "you don't have to pay me back for anything. I've helped you because I love you. You're my family. That's what families do for each other."

Her sister's brow creased. "Well, it's pretty one-sided. I won't continue to be a leach. If you'll still have me, I promise to help. I'll pay rent, buy groceries and find a way to work and go to school. I have a child to raise. I want her to be proud of her mama." Tears slipped down Brittany's cheeks. "I want to be her mama."

"And you will." Jenna stroked her sister's arm.

A knock sounded on the door.

Cliff opened it to find Detective Schwope.

"Is it all right if I come in and speak with Miss Berry?" he asked.

Cliff glanced over his shoulder. "Detective Schwope wants to talk with you, Brittany. Are you up to it?"

Brittany exchanged a glance with Jenna and then nodded. "Yes. Let him in."

Detective Schwope entered, pulling a notepad and pen out of his pocket. "I know you answered a lot of questions last night, but I wanted to check in and see if you remembered anything else about the attack."

Brittany closed her eyes. "It happened so fast."

"It might help if you talk through what happened before the attack," the detective said, his tone gentle.

"Start just before I left the room," Jenna suggested.

"Okay." Brittany kept her eyes closed. "Nurse Grey brought Nurse Smalls in at shift change. Angie said paperwork had to be filled out in Admissions." She opened her eyes and looked at Jenna. "The nurses left, and you walked out of the room shortly after. The baby was sleeping, and I wanted to use the toilet. I thought about buzzing the nurse but was too embarrassed to ask for help to...you know...

"I was only in there for a minute. Everything was too hard to manage on my own, so I was coming out to call for a nurse.

"As soon as I left the bathroom, I was hit in the face with something flat and rectangular."

"The dinner tray," Jenna supplied.

"I fell backward, hit the wall and slid down it. He kept hitting me," she said, her body trembling.

"Did you see his face?" the detective asked.

She shook her head. "All I saw was that tray coming at me over and over."

"Did he say anything?"

"No. He just hit me until I must've passed out."

"You think it was the janitor..." the detective started, "why?"

"I couldn't see his face, but I saw a brief glimpse of gray pants and shirt." Her brow wrinkled. "I remember a janitor walking by my room earlier in a gray coverall."

Jenna nodded. "I saw a janitor in a gray coverall going through the stairwell door as I was coming off the elevator right before Brittany came out of the room crying for help. As soon as she told me what happened, I ran after him. But it was too late. He was gone before I could catch up to him."

"Had you contacted the baby's father?" the detective asked.

Brittany's brow drew into a stubborn line. "No. He wanted to give her up for adoption. He wasn't going to help me if I kept her, so I left him."

"Any chance he could've changed his mind?" the detective persisted.

"I doubt it," Brittany said. "He has a family in Salt Lake City, complete with a wife and kids. I'm sure his wife wouldn't want to take in his bastard child. She probably doesn't even know he has a lover."

"You told one of the other detectives that you'd worked out a deal with a local citizen that, if he paid for your room and board, you'd let him adopt your baby."

Brittany pressed her palms to her cheeks. "He could afford everything a child could want and need. I thought my baby would be better off with him and his wife than with me. I have no money, no education to fall back on, no home. I couldn't give my baby the life she deserved." She looked down at her arms. "But when they put her in my arms..." Brittany shook her head, tears slipping down her cheeks, "I knew I couldn't give her away." She looked up, a fierce scowl on her face. "I would find a way to give her everything she needed. Mostly, I would love her with all my heart. I never want her to think her mother didn't want her."

"Did you inform Mr. Waters that you changed your mind?" the detective asked.

She shook her head, her gaze going to Jenna. "No. I called my sister and asked her to let him know."

The detective turned to Jenna. "Did you tell Mr. Waters of your sister's intention?"

"No, sir," Jenna said. "I haven't had the opportunity. The baby was stolen soon after I arrived."

The detective turned to Cliff. "Where did you come in?"

Cliff shot a glance toward Jenna. "I ran into Special Agent Jenkins in the stairwell on the second floor as she was descending."

"Did you see someone in a gray coverall in the stairwell?" Schwope asked.

"No. Only Miss Jenkins," Cliff said.

The detective closed his notebook. "We had a state policeman go to the address you gave us in Billings. No one was home."

"I'm not surprised," Brittany said. "Larry's probably on the road for his job or back in Salt Lake City with his wife and kids."

"We asked the landlord to give us a call if he shows up anytime soon. We've also put a BOLO out on him to bring him in for questioning."

Brittany's brow furrowed. "BOLO?"

"Sorry," the detective said. "Short for *be on the lookout.*"

Brittany smirked. "I hope they drag him into a police station and scare him good. He played me for far too long."

"Thank you, Miss Berry. I have a few more people to interview while I'm here if you think of anything else. We found the truck we think the baby might have been smuggled out in abandoned behind some warehouses."

Brittany's eyes widened. "And?"

The detective shook his head. "If the baby was in the truck, she wasn't when it was found. We're checking for fingerprints."

Brittany's shoulders sagged. "My poor baby. What a horrible welcome into the real world. She has to be terrified."

"I'm sorry, Miss Berry. We'll do our best to get her back to you as soon as possible."

"Thank you," Jenna said.

As the detective turned to leave, Nurse Grey entered the room, her forehead creased in a frown. "They told me what happened after I left last night." She hurried over to Brittany's side. "I'm so sorry. Nothing like this has ever happened in this hospital. I can't imagine how anyone could walk out with a newborn. We have so many checks in place." She pressed her hand over her mouth, shaking her head from side to side. "Is there anything I can do for you? Anything I can get you?"

Brittany held out her hand. "No, Nurse Grey. Not unless you can get my baby back for me."

The nurse took her hand and held it for a moment. "If I could, I would. But I'm sure the police are on it." She looked around at all the people in the room. "Have they identified a suspect?"

"We have a person of interest in mind but have yet to locate him," the detective said. "You're one of the people I wanted to interview today. You left before Miss Berry was attacked last night, correct?"

"I did," Nurse Grey said. "How can I help?"

"Did you see anyone on the floor that shouldn't have been around? Someone lurking or looking suspicious?"

Nurse Grey shook her head. "All I can recall is the patients, their family members and staff."

"Is it normal for maintenance to clean floors or collect linens late in the evening?" the detective asked.

"As you might guess, giving birth and caring for new mothers can be...messy." Nurse Grey nodded toward Brittany with a smile. "We try to keep things clean. So, yes, maintenance could've been called to clean a room or mop a floor. Why do you ask?"

"Did you notice a maintenance man working in the hallway last night before you left?" he asked.

The older nurse's brow dipped low. "I believe so."

"Did anyone call for maintenance to do a clean-up before you left?" the detective asked.

Nurse Grey pressed a hand to her chest. "I didn't, but someone else might have. Do you want me to check?"

"No, thank you, Nurse Grey," Detective Schwope said. "I've spoken to the other staff members who were on duty last night. No one called for maintenance."

"That's odd because I could swear that I saw someone wearing a hospital maintenance coverall working on this floor last night before I left."

"If you think of anything that didn't seem right or looked out of place last night, please call me at this number." He handed her his business card, gave a curt nod to the others in the room and left.

Nurse Grey stared down at the card. "What is this world coming to?" She looked up at Brittany. "I know when you came in to deliver your baby, you said that you were considering putting her up for adoption, and then you changed your mind..." She shook her head. "This must be so very hard for you. How are you holding up?"

Brittany's eyes filled with tears. "I want my baby back," she said with a sob. "I didn't realize how much I loved her until I held her in my arms. She's a part of me and always will be."

Nurse Grey gave her a sad look. "I'm so sorry."

"It's not your fault," Brittany said. "You weren't even here."

"Maybe if I'd stayed later, this wouldn't have happened."

"You can't blame yourself," Jenna said. "Someone else took the baby. That's who the police will find."

The nurse pressed a hand to her mouth. "Just know, my heart hurts for you. I truly believe everything will work out, and you'll have your baby back soon." She backed out of the room, still frowning, her lips pressed together in a tight line.

"She was so kind when I came in. I was so scared.

She helped me through my labor," Brittany said. "The world needs more Nurse Greys."

Another knock sounded on the door.

"I get the feeling this room is Grand Central Station," Cliff murmured.

"I don't want to talk to another detective," Brittany said. "I've told them the same story over and over."

Cliff opened the door enough to see who was there.

He recognized Hank Patterson immediately and the beautiful blonde standing beside him.

Cliff grinned and turned back to Brittany. "It's not a detective. I think you might want to talk to these folks." He opened the door wider, allowing the two people to enter as he introduced them. "Brittany, Jenna," Cliff said, "this is Hank Patterson and his wife, Sadie McClain."

Jenna stood and held out her hand. "Mr. Patterson, I've heard a lot about you and Brotherhood Protectors."

Hank shook her hand. "All good, I hope."

"Absolutely." Jenna grinned as she turned to his wife. "Ms. McClain, I don't think a soul on earth wouldn't recognize you. It's a pleasure to meet you." Jenna shook the woman's hand and moved aside for the couple to step up to Brittany's bedside. "This is my sister Brittany."

Brittany's eyes widened as Sadie McClain stepped

into her view. "You're...you're Sadie McClain. The movie star."

Sadie smiled, took Brittany's hand in hers and covered it with her other hand. "I am. It's a pleasure to meet you, Brittany. I only wish it were under happier circumstances."

Brittany's eyes filled, spilling more tears down her cheeks. "You heard?"

Sadie nodded, her smile disappearing. "It's why we came."

"When I told Sadie about the stolen baby and the threat to you and your sister," Hank said, "she insisted on coming."

Still holding Brittany's hand, Sadie sank into the seat beside her bed. "I know how I'd feel if one of my babies went missing. I'd be beside myself with worry. Inconsolable."

Brittany nodded wordlessly.

"I also know it takes time to recover from giving birth, having done it twice now." Sadie tossed a quick smile over her shoulder at her husband. "You need a place where you can recuperate in peace without worrying that someone might hurt you."

"I'll be at my sister's house," Brittany said.

"And she'll be investigating the case of your missing baby," Cliff said. "Which means she'll be away from the house most of the day, leaving you alone."

Brittany nodded. "I can take care of myself."

"We understand your sister was attacked in front of her house early this morning," Hank said.

Brittany's gaze shot to Jenna's. "The brick?"

Jenna nodded.

Cliff's gaze met Jenna's. "Hank asked if we needed additional help protecting you and your sister. Neither of you were available to answer. I told him yes. We could use another person to look out for Brittany while Jenna and I search for the baby."

Sadie gave Brittany a gentle smile. "When Hank said he was sending someone else to help, I thought how I'd feel if a strange man came to protect me right after birthing a baby." She shook her head. "I said absolutely not." Sadie gave Cliff a tight smile. "You had the right intentions, but Brittany needs a woman's help in a safe environment." She squeezed Brittany's hand. "We want you to stay with us at White Oak Ranch until they find your baby and catch the man responsible."

Cliff met the accusing frowns of the sisters and shrugged. "It wasn't my idea, but it makes sense."

CHAPTER 7

JENNA'S INSTINCT was to say, *Hell no.* But she tamped down that gut reaction and asked in a reasonable tone, "Just where is this ranch?"

Brittany stared at her sister. "You're not considering this, are you?"

"I want to hear them out before we make a decision," Jenna reasoned.

"Outside Eagle Rock," Hank said.

"Nestled in the beautiful Crazy Mountains," Sadie added. "It's between forty-five minutes and an hour from here." She gave Hank a small frown. "We made it in forty-five. Hank's foot was a little heavy on the accelerator."

Hank nodded. "Look, I can stay and provide security, or Brittany can come back with us where she'll be safe on the ranch. It's our Brotherhood Protectors headquarters with a state-of-the-art security system, monitored twenty-four-seven. She'll be safe there."

"And I'll be there to help her should she need it," Sadie said. "Not some muscle-bound man who wouldn't know the first thing about postpartum care."

"But you're...you're," Brittany shook her head, "Sadie McClain, a huge star who could have as many servants waiting on you as you want. Why would you want to do this?"

Sadie smiled gently. "I wasn't always a big star. I grew up on a ranch, helped wrangle cattle, delivered my share of breach calves and foals and two children of my own. I never forget my roots, and I'm not a bit squeamish."

Hank nodded. "True. I've seen her stick her arm inside a cow to turn a breech calf when the vet couldn't get there in time. I'm not sure I could've done it."

Sadie rolled her eyes. "It helps to have smaller arms," she said. "Not that we're going to run into anything like that in your recovery. I just know how it feels to be the target of someone bent on destroying my life. It's terrifying. I promise you'll be safe on the ranch, and I truly want to help."

Hank nodded. "I told her I would bring you back, but Sadie insisted on coming along."

"I love my husband, but you needed to hear this from a woman who cares." She held Brittany's hand

and reached for Jenna's with her free hand. "I promise we'll take good care of your sister. It will free you of worry for her and give you a chance to find the asshole who took her baby."

Jenna liked this woman. "As much as I'd like to have my sister close where I could keep an eye on her, you make some valid points."

Brittany shook her head. "I want to be close to my baby. If they take me into the Crazy Mountains, I'll be so far away."

"We don't know where your baby is," Jenna said. "I need time and the freedom of worry to find her. If you're with Hank and Sadie, I won't be worrying about you. I can focus and, hopefully, find the baby faster."

"Tell you what," Hank said. "I know a guy with a helicopter. When they find the baby, I'll have them fly her and your sister out to us. It'll be faster than driving across Bozeman at rush hour." He grinned. "Okay, that might be stretching it, but it'll be faster than driving to the ranch."

Brittany's gaze met and held Jenna's. "I don't want to go."

"I know, sweetie," Jenna said. "It's your decision."

Her sister heaved a sigh. "But, if it helps you to focus on finding my baby, I will."

Jenna nodded, a sense of relief washing over her. Her sister would be safe in Hank Patterson's care with the female assistance she'd need in her recovery.

She smiled at Brittany. "Just think of the stories you can tell Baby Blakely someday about staying at a famous movie star's ranch."

"We can do one better," Sadie said. "We can have all of you out to the ranch to stay whenever you like."

Brittany smiled at Sadie. "Thank you."

Sadie patted her hand and stood. "Now all we have to do is get a doctor in here to declare you fit to travel. And don't worry. We'll wait for you if he says you need another night or two in the hospital."

Brittany frowned. "What about *your* children? Don't you need to be home for them tonight?"

Sadie slid her arm around Hank's waist and leaned against him. "I have one of the best babysitters willing to jump in and watch my babies at the drop of a hat."

Hank nodded. "Chuck is one of my protectors. The man has a magic touch with children. I'd trust him with their lives, and they love him. Whenever he has them for a night or two, it's one big slumber party. They might prefer we don't come right home, just for a chance to hang with Chuck."

"But they'd be happy for us to be home tonight with a special guest," Sadie added. "We'll let the doctor decide what's best for his patient."

As if on cue, the doctor stepped through the door and glanced around at the number of people in the room. She cocked an eyebrow. "Are we having a party, and I didn't get the memo?"

"No, ma'am," Cliff said. "We're just waiting for you to tell us if Miss Brittany is fit to leave."

The doctor crossed her arms over her chest. "Then how about everyone but Brittany leave the room so I can examine the patient?"

"Going," Hank said, pressing a hand to the small of his wife's back.

Sadie smiled at Brittany. "We'll be back as soon as the doctor completes her evaluation."

"Thank you," Brittany said.

Jenna stood and would have walked out with the others, but Brittany grasped her arm. "Stay," she whispered.

Jenna glanced toward the doctor. "I'm Brittany's sister. She wants me to stay."

"That's fine," the doctor said. "The rest of these people need to give my patient some privacy."

Hank and Sadie stepped out of the room.

Cliff met Jenna's gaze. "I'll be right outside the door if you need me."

"Thanks," Jenna said. "We'll be fine."

Hank held the door for Sadie and Cliff.

As Cliff passed Hank, he asked, "Did Gus's ride make it?"

Hank nodded. "Hannah and Gavin came—"

The door swung closed behind them, leaving Jenna and Brittany with the doctor.

"I'm Dr. Jackson." The doctor stepped up to the bedside and pulled a penlight from her pocket, which she shined into Brittany's eyes one at a time. "I wasn't on duty last night, but I heard about an attack, and your baby was taken. I'm so sorry this happened to you." She was all business, checking Brittany's injuries.

Jenna turned her back while the doctor checked Brittany's lower region, asking about pain, and if she'd gotten up to walk yet.

Brittany snorted. "I got up to use the toilet last night. That's when I was attacked."

"I'd like you to make a trip down the hallway and back without any problems before you leave. But other than that, I see no need for you to stay another night in the hospital unless you're uncomfortable leaving so soon."

Jenna turned back as the doctor smoothed the sheets back over Brittany's legs. "If my sister leaves the hospital, is she up for an hour-long drive to where she'll be staying?"

The doctor nodded. "She should be all right as long as she picks up her prescriptions before she leaves." The doctor's brow dipped. "I hope they find your baby soon. I'm so sorry this has happened to you. The hospital staff are working with the police to help find your baby. I pray it's soon." As the doctor exited, Hank, Sadie and Cliff came back in.

"What was the doctor's verdict?" Sadie asked.

"I have to run a marathon to the end of the hallway and back before they'll release me." Brittany sighed. "And it appears I'm okay for a trip to your ranch."

Jenna reached for Brittany's hand. "You don't have to go if you don't want to."

"That's right," Hank said. "I'll stay and keep you safe here in Bozeman."

"And I could stay for a couple of days to help," Sadie offered. "Chuck was warned we could be away for a day or two."

Brittany's gaze locked on Jenna's. "No. It's better if I'm out of the picture for a while. I want all the focus here in Bozeman to be on finding my baby, not taking care of me." She gave Sadie a weak smile. "If you're sure I won't be too much of a bother, I'll go with you to your ranch until the baby's found and the person who attacked me and my sister is caught."

Jenna squeezed her sister's hand, happy she'd be well protected but sad that she wouldn't be nearby.

"I was looking forward to some sister time," Brittany said with a crooked smile.

"It's going to happen," Jenna assured her. "And I can't wait to work on my auntie skills with Baby Blakely." She looked around. "Now, we have to get you up for that marathon."

Brittany shook her head. "No. You're not going to help me. Nurse Grey can do that. I'd rather you go by my apartment over the bar to collect some of my clothes, brush and toiletries to take with me to Hank and Sadie's."

"I can do both," Jenna said. "I'm sure the release orders will take time."

Brittany shook her head. "I don't want to keep Hank and Sadie waiting any longer than they have to."

"Sweetie," Sadie smiled, "don't worry about us. Take your time. In fact, I can help you up and down the hallway if you like."

"Only if Nurse Grey can't do it," Brittany said. "You're just a little thing. And I'm...well...bigger. Especially with the baby weight. And you're..." Brittany waved a hand. "You're Sadie McClain. What if I fall on you and hurt you?"

Sadie planted her fists on her hips. "Honey, we need to get something straight. I'm just a ranch girl from Eagle Rock, Montana. I can handle a lot more than you think."

Hank nodded. "People underestimate her all the time." He grinned at his wife. "She's strong enough to toss an eighty-pound hay bale and never gets tired. I can't keep up with her."

Brittany's brow wrinkled skeptically. "I'm sorry. It'll take some getting used to. I've been taking care of myself for so long that I hate relying on anyone else. And I don't want to be a burden on anyone."

Jenna brushed a strand of her sister's hair back from her forehead. "You're never a burden, love."

Brittany tapped the call button for the nurse. "If

Nurse Grey doesn't have time to help, you're on, Ms. McClain."

"Sadie," the movie star said with a wink.

A young nurse Jenna hadn't seen before pushed through the door and stopped when confronted by all the people in the room. "Oh, hello, I'm Nurse Haddox," she said, her attention going to Brittany. "Did you need something?"

"Do you have time to walk me to the end of the hallway and back?" Brittany asked.

Nurse Haddox bit her lip. "I'm in the middle of dispensing medications. Could you wait for thirty minutes?"

Brittany frowned. "Is Nurse Grey available?"

The young nurse shook her head. "No. She had to go home to take care of her mother. We're a little short on staff. But I can help you in thirty minutes."

Sadie stepped forward. "It's okay. I can help her. You do what you need to do."

Nurse Haddox looked from Sadie to Brittany. "If you're okay with that, I'll be in and out of rooms in the hallway if you have any problems."

"Thank you, Ms. Haddox," Sadie said. "We'll be okay. Right, Brittany?"

Brittany nodded.

Nurse Haddox sighed. "Thank you." And she hurried out of the room.

"If you're good for now, I'll go to your apartment and pack a bag," Jenna said.

"You go," Hank said. "We'll ensure Brittany runs her marathon and gets all her discharge papers in order." His gaze shifted to Cliff.

Cliff nodded. "We'll be back as quickly as possible."

"Oh, and Jenna..." Brittany called out.

"Yes," Jenna turned back.

She motioned for Jenna to come close and whispered. "Mr. Water's business card is in the top drawer of the nightstand, sticking out of the pages of a book I was reading. It has his name, David Waters, on the front with his work phone and address. His home address and personal cell phone number are handwritten on the back, along with the amount he gave me and what he promised upon delivery. I know the police have probably already interviewed him, but if he's not the one who took my baby, I owe him the courtesy of telling him I'd changed my mind anyway. He might still expect me to give her up for adoption once she's found."

Jenna nodded. "He's one of the people I want to talk to. I'll be sure to let him know."

"Cleaning up my messes again," Brittany said, her lips twisting. "I love you, Jenna."

Jenna hugged her. "Love you, too." Anxious to get to the apartment and get back, she left the room with Cliff on her heels.

After the incident with the brick through her window earlier, Jenna was glad Cliff was going with her. She felt confident Brittany was being taken care of, which helped reduce the worry and left her free to focus on finding the baby.

Once they left the hospital, Jenna headed for her car.

"Let's take my truck," Cliff said.

She grimaced. "Right. I don't imagine you want to sit on all the glass in my front seat."

"Not particularly."

Riding shotgun, Jenna gave Cliff directions to the bar. Still early in the day, the bar wasn't open. Jenna found a staircase on the side of the building and climbed up to the door at the top, Cliff bringing up the rear.

When she reached out to place the key in the lock, she noticed the door wasn't closed all the way.

Cliff grabbed her wrist. "Let me go first."

Jenna shook her head. "I'm trained to clear a building, and I have a gun," she said, pulling her weapon out of the holster.

"Right," he said, "but I'm right behind you."

Jenna stood to the side of the door, out of range if someone was on the other side. With the barrel of her Glock, she nudged the door open and peered around the doorframe into the dark interior of the apartment.

Reaching a hand inside, she felt for the light switch and flipped it on. A single bulb hanging from the ceiling cast a yellow glow throughout the small room.

It appeared as if a tornado had swept through, stirring the contents of the room, flinging everything across every available surface.

Nothing moved inside, and there wasn't anywhere to hide in a space barely big enough for a twin-sized bed, a dorm refrigerator and a small counter with a sink and a hotplate.

Picking her way through the mess, Jenna found a door on one wall that led into a bathroom with a shower that belonged in a camp trailer, a toilet and a pedestal sink.

Jenna lowered her weapon, her heart sinking into her belly. "I can't believe my sister lived here during the last couple weeks of her pregnancy." She shook her head. "The stairs alone had to have been awful. And the shower..." She stepped out of the bathroom and looked around the room.

"She's pretty tough," Cliff said, ducking his head into the bathroom. "But yeah, I can't imagine anyone getting into or out of that shower easily. Especially someone who was nine months pregnant." He shook his head. "It looks like someone came through here looking for something."

"We can't move anything, and be careful not to touch anything." Jenna holstered her weapon and pulled out her cell phone to call the detective.

He answered on the first ring. "Schwope here. Whatcha got, Jenkins?"

"I'm at my sister's apartment. It's been tossed."

"I'll send someone over to dust for prints. Anything missing?"

Jenna shrugged. "No idea. She didn't have much. I can't imagine there was anything here worth stealing. I need to get back to the hospital."

"Dispatch tells me there's a unit around the corner if you can wait until he gets there."

"Will do," Jenna said. As she waited, her gaze swept over the few pieces of furniture and came to rest on the nightstand. She fished in her jacket pocket for surgical gloves, pulled them on and then picked her way across the floor to the drawer hanging slightly open.

"I thought you said we shouldn't touch anything?" Cliff said.

Jenna nodded. "That's why I carry gloves." She pulled the drawer open a little more and looked inside. A book lay amid a few socks and T-shirts. She lifted it and thumbed through the pages. "Before I left Brittany, she asked me to look for a business card she'd stuck between the pages of a book inside her nightstand." Jenna stopped thumbing through and turned the book over, fanning the pages. Nothing fell out.

At that moment, a police officer arrived at the

door of the apartment. "Special Agent Jenkins?" he asked, looking at Cliff.

Cliff tipped his head toward Jenna.

"That's me." Jenna laid the book on the nightstand and nodded to the officer. "When they're collecting prints, make sure they check for prints on this book." She shot a glance toward Cliff. "Ready?"

He nodded. "I take it you're not going to pack a bag for your sister."

She shook her head. What was there wasn't worth worrying about and would be tied up until they got all the fingerprints they wanted. "Not from here. We'll stop by my house for a few things and at a store on the way back."

Once in Cliff's truck, Cliff started the engine and looked over at Jenna. "Whose business card?"

Jenna's jaw tightened. "Mr. Waters. The man who gave her money and promised more when she delivered the baby."

CHAPTER 8

WITH JENNA'S DIRECTIONS, Cliff drove to her cottage and went up to the door with her.

The fierce barking on the other side made him smile. "I wonder if the person who threw the brick had come to your house intent on breaking in like they did at Brittany's apartment."

"I'd wondered the same," Jenna said as she unlocked the door and uttered a command. "Sit."

A dark sable German shepherd sat back on his haunches, eying Cliff.

"Good boy," Jenna said. "His bark is wicked, but he's usually friendly with friendly people."

Cliff frowned. "I know I'm friendly. Will *he* know I'm friendly?"

She shrugged. "Let him sniff your hand and find out." Jenna grinned. "What have you got to lose?"

"My hand?" he said. Respectful of the animal, Cliff

dropped to a squat and slowly extended his hand toward the dog, his fingers curled in case the animal decided to bite.

"His name is Brutus," Jenna said, her hand smoothing down the dog's back.

Brutus sniffed his hand, seemed to look Cliff in the eye and then licked his knuckles.

Cliff laughed. "I guess that means I passed the sniff test?"

Jenna smiled. "You did." She turned and walked through a living room.

Cliff followed, the dog falling in step beside him, tail wagging. He reached down and scratched behind Brutus's ear. "Good dog."

Jenna disappeared down a hallway into a bedroom.

"Need any help?"

"No. I'm just going to pack a few things for Brittany. She's shorter and normally a size smaller than I am, but some of my things will fit her until I can get her things from her apartment, or we can go shopping for new clothes."

The living room was furnished with an off-white sofa and two side chairs in a light teal. The furniture didn't look new but was well cared for.

"Do you own or rent this house?" Cliff asked.

"Own," she answered from the bedroom. "Or rather, the bank owns it until I pay it off. I have it on a fifteen-year loan, but I hope to pay it off earlier. What about you? Are you a homeowner?"

He laughed. "No. I was never in one place long enough. It didn't make sense to buy a house I wasn't going to live in." But he'd saved his money, knowing that when he left the Navy, he'd buy a house and put down roots.

Jenna emerged from her bedroom, wheeling a suitcase behind her. "Now that you're not in the Navy, are you going to buy a house?"

He shrugged. "Probably."

She stopped in front of him and glanced around the living room. "Just don't go small. I thought this cottage was all I needed." She shook her head. "With Brittany and Baby Blakely moving in...I might have to find a bigger place. One with two bathrooms. I don't know how long we'll last with three females fighting over one bathroom." She grinned. "But I'm willing to try. I have a niece." Jenna's eyes narrowed as she met his gaze. "And we *will* bring her home."

He reached out and brushed his thumb along her chin. "Yes, we will." Then, as natural as it was to breathe, he pressed a kiss to her lips.

Jenna touched her fingers to her lips. "Why did you do that?"

"I don't know," he said. "It just felt right."

She frowned.

"Sorry. But not really sorry." He stepped back and

held up his hands. "I won't do it again if it makes you uncomfortable."

She stared at him a moment longer, then dropped her hand to the suitcase handle. "We'd better get going. I want to make one more stop before we head back to the hospital."

Cliff followed her out and waited on the porch as she patted Brutus once more and then locked the door.

He fought the urge to smile. He'd given her the opportunity to tell him to knock it off with the kissing.

She hadn't told him to stop.

Kissing her had felt good and right. He wondered how much better it would feel if she kissed him back.

They stopped at a ladies' undergarment store on the way back. Cliff remained in the truck while Jenna went in. Less than ten minutes later, she came out carrying a relatively small pink bag with pink tissues poking out of the top.

"You didn't buy much," he noted as he shifted into drive and pulled out of the parking lot onto the road.

"Though expensive, ladies' panties don't take up much space, unlike men's boxer shorts or briefs."

"True." He headed for the hospital. "Any more stops?"

She shook her head. "No. Though I hate to see my sister leave, I'm ready to get on with this investigation. I'm glad she'll be with Hank and Sadie in a safe environment while we chase any leads we can find."

At the hospital, they left the bags in the truck, checked in with the front desk and made their way up to the third floor.

When they entered Brittany's room, the new mother was seated in a wheelchair, wearing a baggy maternity dress and tennis shoes. Her hair was neatly combed and pulled back in a braid, and she held a sheath of papers in her lap.

"Finally. I've received my discharge papers, and I'm ready to go," she said and frowned. "You didn't bring my things?"

Jenna's lips twisted. "No...and yes."

Brittany tilted her head. "I don't understand."

Jenna told her what they'd found at her apartment and how they'd had to leave it for the crime scene investigators to dust for prints. "I'll go back later and collect your belongings once the room has been processed."

"Why would someone break into my apartment and throw my stuff around? It's not like I have anything nice. I don't even have any jewelry worth stealing." Her eyes narrowed. "Did you find my book?"

Jenna nodded. "I did."

Brittany leaned forward. "And?"

"Nothing inside," Jenna said.

"I know it was there. I put it there yesterday

before I came to the hospital." Brittany bounced her fist on the armrest of the wheelchair. "I remember specifically placing it between the pages."

"It wasn't there," Jenna said. "But don't worry. Bozeman isn't that big. I'll find him and pass on your message. We'll go with you out to Hank's vehicle. I packed some of my clothes for you. As soon as I can, I'll get yours to you."

"Better still," Brittany said, "find my baby, and you won't have to get my clothes to me. I'll come home."

"That's the plan." Jenna nodded toward Hank and Sadie. "And if you think of anything that will help us find who took Blakely, let Hank know. He's got a network of people who can help us find the man who took her. It's what his organization does."

Brittany nodded. "Trust me. I've gone over everything that happened yesterday, from the moment I arrived at the hospital to the attack. But if I think of anything, I'll let him know."

Hank handed Jenna the backpack she'd left there earlier. She slung it over her shoulder and gripped the wheelchair handles.

Cliff held the door open for everyone to go through.

"I'll drive," said a young woman wearing scrubs and a badge identifying her as a medical assistant. "Hospital rules."

Jenna stepped aside and let the woman push the wheelchair.

They all crowded into the elevator, descended to ground level and went out the exit used for picking up patients. Hank hurried to get the SUV and drove it around to the pickup point.

Cliff retrieved the suitcase and the pink bag while Jenna waited with the others at Hank's SUV.

She hugged her sister and helped Brittany into the back seat. "Take care of yourself. Blakely is going to need you at one hundred percent."

"I will," she said. "And Jenna, thank you for being the best big sister. I'm sorry I haven't been the best little sister. I'll do better. I promise."

"You're perfect as you are," Jenna said. "And you're going to be a great mom to that baby girl."

Brittany gave her a sad smile. "I hope so."

Cliff loaded the suitcase and pink bag into the back of the SUV,

As they drove away, Jenna heaved a big sigh. "Let's get to work. We're going to find that baby."

He walked with her to his truck and held open her door.

Once she was inside, he rounded to the driver's side, got in and started the engine. "Where to?"

"I want to talk with Mr. David Waters."

He grinned. "I thought you'd want to start there. I called Swede a minute ago and had him look up the man's home and business address. He texted both to me." Cliff pointed to his truck's screen display of a map. "Since it's a weekday, I'm betting he's at his office. I've already input the address on my map app."

Jenna leaned back in her seat. "I have my resources as well," she said. "But thanks for being a step ahead. Did Swede have anything on Larry Sutton?"

"He's working on it. There isn't much information on Larry Sutton in Billings, Montana, other than his driver's license on file with the DMV." Cliff shook his head. "He's having to dig deeper. He looked for a Larry Sutton in Salt Lake City, but none of them look like the photo I sent."

Jenna pulled out her cell phone and dialed a number.

"Who are you calling?" Cliff asked.

"Detective Schwope," she answered briefly before focusing on the call. "Yes, she was released a few minutes ago. No, she won't be staying with me. If you need to get in touch with her, call me first. I'll let her know." She shifted the cell phone to her other ear. "Has anyone gone to Billings to check out the baby daddy?" She paused. "Not there? Did they go in to see if there was any evidence of a baby being there? They did?" Her lips thinned. "Nothing... Did they lift prints?" She nodded. "Good. Hopefully, it will help us identify this guy. I have a feeling Larry Sutton is an alias. Not his real name. Thanks. I'll get online and see if I can find a match with the prints and using facial recognition." She paused again. "I'll keep you informed. Thank you."

"They got fingerprints from the ex-boyfriend's apartment?" Cliff asked.

"They did. That will only help if he's in a military or criminal database." She glanced at Cliff. "You say your guy Swede can tap into almost any information found on the internet?"

"I'm not sure what databases he can access, but he finds a way, from what I hear." Cliff glanced over at Jenna. "Why?"

"While we're interviewing Waters, see if he can tap into the NGI-IPS, Next Generation Identification-Interstate Photo System to find a match on the photo you sent." Jenna stared straight ahead. "I might be able to get access, but it could take time, and we could be talking to suspects while a computer is searching for the match."

Cliff's lip turned up on one corner. "Are you asking him to break the rules and potentially hack into this system?"

Jenna lifted her chin and refused to meet his gaze. "I have no idea what you're talking about."

Cliff chuckled. "Gotcha." As he steered with one hand, he called Swede with the other and relayed the request without saying it was from Jenna.

"Already on it," Swede replied. "Takes time, though, for the application to go through potentially thirty million photos. I'll let you know what, if anything, I find."

"Thanks, Swede."

"Anything to bring that kid home," Swede said and ended the call.

Cliff turned into a parking lot of an office building with a sign advertising a number of different businesses, including one David Waters, Certified Financial Planner.

He parked and met Jenna at the front of the truck. Together, they entered the building and rode the elevator up to the floor where Waters' office was located.

A secretary looked up as they entered through a glass door and smiled. "May I help you?"

"Is Mr. Waters in?" Jenna asked.

The secretary's eyebrows rose. "Do you have an appointment?"

Jenna flipped out her badge. "FBI Special Agent Jenkins. I'd like to speak with Mr. Waters, please."

The woman studied the badge, her eyes narrowing. Finally, she said. "Let me see if he's available."

She touched a button on her desk phone and lifted the receiver, pressing it to her ear. "Mr. Waters, there's an FBI Agent here who'd like to speak with you." She nodded. "Yes, sir." After she placed the receiver on its cradle, she smiled up at Jenna and waved a hand toward the door behind her. "Mr. Waters will see you."

Jenna strode past the secretary's desk. As she reached for the door handle, the door swung inward. A tall, slim man in a tailored, charcoal-gray suit stood just inside.

He backed up a step and said, "Please, come in."

Once Jenna and Cliff were through the door, Mr. Waters closed it behind them. He faced Jenna and Cliff and held out his hand. "I'm David Waters."

Jenna took the hand and gave it a brief shake. "Special Agent Jenkins." She tipped her head toward Cliff. "And this is Cliff Cranston."

After they all shook hands, Waters waved them further into the spacious office, indicating a seating area by the window with a sofa and two chairs grouped around a low coffee table. "Please, have a seat."

Jenna perched on the edge of the sofa.

Cliff sat beside her.

Mr. Waters landed on one of the chairs. "Are you here because of the missing baby?"

Jenna nodded. "We are."

Waters shook his head. "I talked with a detective last night and told him I don't have the baby. I didn't even know the young lady had gone into labor until the detective showed up at my home."

"Can you tell us where you were at approximately nine-thirty yesterday evening?" Jenna asked.

He sighed. "As I told the detective, I was playing poker with friends. I even gave him the names and phone numbers of the guys. Have they contacted them for verification?"

"I'll check with them when I leave here," Jenna said. "Did you offer to buy Brittany Berry's baby?"

Cliff was almost as jolted by Jenna's question as Waters was. It switched directions so fast and posed the question in such a way as to throw the man off balance.

Waters ran a hand through his hair. "Look, I did not target Ms. Berry and offer to buy her baby. It all started as a polite question. I asked when her baby was due." He sighed. "I felt sorry for her, standing behind that bar, looking ready to pop at any minute."

"So, you offered to buy her baby to help her out?" Jenna persisted.

Waters leaned his elbows on his knees and clasped his hands together. "My wife and I have been married for nine years and have been trying to have a baby for most of those nine years. I love her with all my heart and would give her anything. But I can't give her the baby she so desperately wants. She's had five miscarriages and one live birth." He looked away, his jaw tight. "Our son was our rainbow baby. Perfect in every way. After all the losses, we finally had a child to love."

Waters paused, loosened his necktie and stared down at his hands. "I was working half-days for two months after we brought the baby home and went back to full days."

He stopped and ran his hand through his hair again. "I'm sorry. I'm making this story longer than you probably even care to listen to. To make it short, I came home one day and asked how the baby was. My wife Trudy said she'd put him down for a nap an hour before. We went into his room together to wake him up." Waters shook his head. "He wouldn't wake up. He lay there like he was asleep—a perfect, cold angel who went to sleep and never woke up. My wife was devastated."

Jenna opened her mouth to say something.

Waters held up his hand. "We talked for a while that evening. Ms. Berry said she couldn't imagine how she'd raise a child when she barely made enough to feed herself and couldn't afford a better place to live than a crummy matchbox of an apartment over a bar."

He looked up, his face haggard. "I told her that if she was serious about putting the baby up for adoption, would she consider me and my wife." He laughed. "She asked for my driver's license, made a copy of it and then asked me to show her my bank accounts to prove I could afford to raise a child."

"Did you know she had gone into labor?" Jenna asked.

Waters shook his head. "If I had known, I might've come to the hospital. The girl didn't have any family or a place to go. At least that's what I thought. Apparently, she has a sister here in Bozeman," he sneered, "for what it's worth. If she'd cared about her sister, she wouldn't have forced her to work at that bar so far into her pregnancy."

Jenna stiffened.

Cliff touched her arm and met her gaze. He hoped to remind her that she was supposed to be an FBI agent, not an avenging sister, looking for someone to blame in the disappearance of her young niece.

Jenn's shoulders sagged. She looked away from Cliff and back at David Waters. "Did you know Ms. Berry had changed her mind about letting you adopt her baby girl?"

Water's head jerked up. "No. I didn't know." His eyebrows met in a deep V over his nose. "She changed her mind?"

Cliff studied the man's expression as a shadow passed over his face.

"I'm sorry to hear that. A healthy, happy baby would've been loved in our home." His mouth twisted into a wry smile. "I didn't tell my wife about the arrangement because I couldn't face her disappointment if it fell through. To build up her hopes, only for the mother to keep the baby, would've been too cruel. So, I didn't tell her about my arrangement. I was going to wait until Ms. Berry delivered the baby. If it was healthy and Ms. Berry didn't back out, I would've surprised Trudy with the baby."

Jenna snorted. You surprise people with chocolate

or flowers. Maybe even a piece of jewelry. Not a baby.

Waters met and held Jenna's gaze. "I'm glad I didn't tell my wife. I don't think she could take another disappointment. I guess I had a feeling Ms. Berry wouldn't go through with it. Either that or our streak of bad luck would continue despite all our efforts to keep trying. Maybe I'm a pessimist, but I don't think we were meant to have a child of our own."

For a long moment, Jenna stared at the man. Then she pushed to her feet and held out her hand. "Thank you for your time."

Cliff shook hands with the man and followed Jenna out of the posh office and into the bright Texas sunshine.

Jenna stood for a moment, lifting her face to the sun.

Cliff stood a step away from Jenna, wanting to take her into his arms but not wanting to disturb her meditation. "Do you believe him?" he asked.

"That he didn't have anything to do with the kidnapping?" Jenna looked at Cliff. "I don't *want* to believe him. But yes. I don't think he took the baby."

Cliff nodded. "I agree. He didn't appear to be the kind of guy who'd steal a baby. But then, I don't know what that kind of guy should look like."

"Exactly." Jenna pushed her shoulders back.

"Where to next?" Cliff asked.

"I have no idea," A shiver shook her body. "I'm afraid."

Cliff pulled her into his arms and held her body flush against his, a hand stroking her hair. "You're a complete badass. What can you possibly be afraid of?"

"I'm afraid I'll fail in this mission." Her fingers curled into his shirt. "I'm terrified Baby Blakely will be lost forever."

CHAPTER 9

Cliff pulled Jenna into his arms and held her for a long moment. When he set her at arms' length, he met and held her gaze. "Get this straight—we *will* find the baby and bring her back to her mother."

She stared into his eyes. After a long moment, she nodded. "Yes. We will."

He kissed her forehead and stepped away, dropping his arms to his sides. "I think we should go back to Brittany's apartment. If nothing else, we can gather her things to take to your house." He glanced at his watch. "If the bar is open, we can talk with the bartender. He might have seen something or maybe the person who ransacked her apartment."

"Good idea." Jenna squared her shoulders and gave him a weak smile. "My apologies. I'm not usually so emotional on a case."

"And you're not usually looking for a stolen baby

belonging to your sister." He touched a hand to the small of her back, guided her back to his truck and handed her up into the passenger seat.

He looked up at her as she adjusted her seatbelt. "All it takes is a single clue. It might come from Swede, your detective, a memory Brittany hasn't divulged or a note scribbled on a napkin. A single clue...and the threads will start unraveling."

She nodded. "I know this. We just have to find that first clue."

"Let's hope it's in her apartment." Cliff rounded the front of his truck and slipped into the driver's seat. Seconds later, they were back on the road, headed for the Bear Claw Tavern and the little apartment above it.

On the drive over, Cliff glanced in the rearview mirror several times as a white sedan kept pace with his truck. When he turned, the sedan turned. When they neared the tavern, the white sedan sped past them, a person wearing a gray hoodie at the wheel. He didn't look toward the truck; he just kept driving.

A few cars were parked in the bar's front parking lot.

Jenna selected a number on her cell phone and raised the device to her ear. "Detective Schwope, Special Agent Jenkins. We're at my sister's apartment. Are we clear to go inside?" She nodded. "Thank you." With a quick glance at Cliff, she pushed open her truck door. "Just wanted to make sure it was okay to go inside. We can."

Cliff chuckled. "Always the rule follower."

"You say that like it's a bad thing," she said.

Cliff grinned as he led the way up the steps to the apartment and held out his hand for the key.

Jenna laid it in his palm and waited as he opened the door.

The small room was no cleaner than the last time they'd been there. In fact, it was decidedly dirtier, with black graphite dust scattered over every smooth surface, including the book she'd left for them to check.

Jenna searched through the mess for something she could use to collect all of Brittany's things. She found a large gym bag and a couple of commercial trash bags her sister must have taken from the bar.

It didn't take long to gather all the clothes. There weren't many. A faded yellow sundress she must have worn as a maternity dress, two pairs of jeans that were still folded over a hanger that had been tossed to the floor and two button-up blouses. One a mint green short-sleeve, the other a blue chambray.

The apartment didn't have a closet or a dresser. The clothes were on hangers that, Jenna assumed, had been hung on a couple of hooks attached to the wall. She found several T-shirts, half a dozen pairs of panties and socks in the drawers of the nightstand. She bent to look beneath the bed and found a pair of snow boots that had seen better days and a puffy gray winter coat with a few tears in the fabric.

Everything fit into the gym bag, including the puffy coat.

Cliff straightened the mattress on the bed frame and gathered the sheets and blanket from the floor.

Jenna held open one of the trash bags while Cliff stuffed the bedclothes in.

With the bed linens and clothing out of the way, there wasn't much left.

Jenna bent to lift a metal picture frame from where it had landed on the floor. When she turned it over, she smiled down at the young girls with their arms around each other, grinning at the photographer.

Cliff leaned over her shoulder, his breath warm against the side of her neck. "You and Brittany?"

She nodded.

"How old were you in the photo?" he asked.

"I was thirteen. Brittany was eight." She stared at the tent in the background. "We'd gone camping on summer vacation. I think it was the last time we had fun as a family. Although, I'm not so sure Mom had as much fun. She didn't much care for camping. Brittany and I had a blast. It wasn't until she turned twelve that she got sassy and rebellious."

Cliff lifted the trash bag full of bedclothes and carried it to the door.

Jenna tucked the photo into the bag with the

clothing. A stack of papers lay on a small rectangular table pushed up against the wall. She gathered the documents and thumbed through them, one at a time, finding an advertisement for an air conditioner repair service, a bill for a doctor's visit, a receipt for a few groceries and a brochure from Little Angel Adoption Agency.

"What did you find?" Cliff asked, coming to stand beside her.

Jenna frowned and held up the document. "A brochure for an adoption agency."

"I thought she'd decided to go with Mr. Waters if she was to give up the baby for adoption."

"Me, too." Jenna opened the pamphlet and checked out the contact information. "That's odd."

"What?"

She turned the brochure over and checked the back. "There isn't an address. Just a phone number."

Cliff took the paper from her hand and looked it over. "That is weird. Just a phone number? Sounds sketchy to me."

She pulled out her cell phone and dialed the number, placing the call on speaker.

After several rings, a female voice came on. "Are you looking for a baby to complete your family? Let Little Angel Adoption Agency help you find the perfect addition. Leave your name and number at the tone. An adoption coordinator will get back to you as soon as possible."

Jenna ended the call before it could start recording a message.

Cliff snapped a photo of the brochure and a closeup of the phone number. "I'm sending this to Swede. He can ask Brittany where she got this and if she contacted the agency about placing her baby up for adoption."

Jenna gave one last look around the small room. "Everything she owns fits in these two bags." She shook her head. "How could I let my only sister get so far beyond my radar?"

"You thought she was in a committed relationship with Larry."

"Never once in any of our phone conversations did she indicate anything was wrong. What bothers me most is that she never told me she was pregnant." Her gaze swept the room, imagining Brittany sitting alone on the twin bed, her belly swollen and her finances at rock bottom. "No wonder she considered placing her baby with someone who could easily give her everything Brittany couldn't."

"She must've felt desperate," Cliff agreed.

She hefted the gym bag and slipped the strap over her shoulder. "Ready to talk to the bar owner?"

Cliff slung the bag of sheets and blankets over his shoulder, opened the door and held it for Jenna.

As she passed by, she smiled up at him. "Thanks for hanging out with me today. If you have anything you need to do, I can handle talking to the tavern owner on my own."

The Navy SEAL dropped the bag of bed clothes and crossed his arms over his broad chest. "If you want me to go...I'll leave." He held up a finger. "I won't like it, but I'll leave."

"I want you to leave," she said and cocked a challenging eyebrow.

Cliff stared at her, his brow wrinkling. "Really?"

Jenna lifted her chin and met his gaze. She opened her mouth with every intention of saying *yes*. "No." Almost as shocked at her answer as he was, her mouth twisted in a wry grin. "No," she repeated. "Strangely enough, I like having you around. And if you aren't busy or don't have anywhere else to be, I'd like you to come with me to talk with the tavern owner."

"Good." Cliff nodded. "Because I would've left... but I wasn't going far. You see, I'm all in on the investigation. I want to bring back Baby Blakely as much as every person involved in this case."

Jenna adjusted the gym bag strap on her shoulder. "Good," she said. "Because we need all the help we can get to find her." Then, without thinking or overthinking, she hooked her free hand around the back of his neck, leaned up on her toes and kissed him full on the lips.

As quickly as it had begun, Jenna ended it and stepped through the door.

"Whoa." Cliff grabbed the bag of sheets and blankets. "You don't kiss a guy like that and just leave."

Her eyes widened. "I did."

He dropped the bag of laundry on the landing and gripped her arms. "Why?"

She shrugged. "I don't know. It just feels natural," she said, echoing what he'd said when he'd kissed her for the second time. Jenna shook free of his grasp and headed down the stairs, warmth spreading throughout her body. The urge to kiss him had come on her so suddenly she hadn't stopped to question it, just reacted.

Her lips still tingled, as well as other parts of her body. How long had it been since she'd been with a man?

Since her breakup with Ryan, the surge of desire Cliff inspired had reawakened her to possibilities she'd thought impossible after her heart and ego had taken such a huge hit.

As she arrived at the bottom of the stairs, she realized anything between her and Cliff would have to go on hold until they found Baby Blakely—all the more reason to focus and get her back as quickly as possible.

They carried Brittany's belongings to Cliff's truck and stowed them in the back seat.

Jenna glanced at her watch. With the end of the work day, the parking lot had more cars and trucks than when they'd started up the stairs to Brittany's apartment. The sun sank low on the horizon, shadows lengthened and streetlights blinked on one by one.

Cliff touched a hand to the small of Jenna's back as they entered the bar.

She liked having him beside her as they stepped through the door into the dimly lit interior. Several television screens mounted on the walls at different angles displayed a variety of sports, from soccer to wrestling, horse racing and golf. In a couple of months, football would fill each screen to the exclusion of all other sports.

Jenna didn't stop until she reached the bar, found two empty stools and slid onto one.

Cliff landed on the one beside her.

An older man with gray hair and a barrel chest stood behind the bar, mixing drinks and filling mugs full of beer.

He laid a glass of whiskey in front of a man seated at the far end of the bar and filled a tray with the beer he'd poured from the tap.

A waitress wearing a tight T-shirt, cutoff shorts and cowboy boots lifted the tray over her right shoulder and carried it to a table in the corner.

The bartender stopped in front of Jenna and Cliff. "What can I getcha?"

Cliff glanced at Jenna.

She smiled at the bartender. "I'll have a beer."

"Bottle or on tap?"

"Tap," she responded.

"Make that two," Cliff said.

As the bartender filled their drink orders, Jenna studied the man.

When he returned with their mugs full of beer, he set the drinks on the bar in front of them.

"Sir," Jenna said, "are you the owner of this tavern."

The man nodded, his lip curling up on one side. "I am." He planted his hands on the counter. "What can I do for you?"

Jenna held out her hand. "I'm Jenna Jenkins, Brittany Berry's sister."

His eyes narrowed. "You're her sister?"

Jenna nodded with a smile. "I know...we don't look much alike."

"No. You don't. Rome Martin." As he took her hand, the tavern owner's brow wrinkled. "I didn't know she had a sister. How is she? I called the ambulance for her last night. Did she have the baby?" He released her hand and wiped a damp rag over the surface of the bar.

"She's doing well enough. Yes, she had the baby. But there was some trouble at the hospital."

The bar owner's hand stilled. "Are she and the baby okay?"

"Brittany's okay," Jenna said. "We're not sure about the baby."

"Oh, hell. What happened?" The man met Jenna's

gaze. "No, wait, I heard something about a missing baby on the news. Please, Lord, don't tell me that baby was Brittany's."

Jenna's lips pressed together in a tight line. "It was."

He shook his head. "What the hell happened?"

"That's what we're trying to figure out," Jenna said.

He grabbed a rag and wiped it across the bar. "She had the baby in her belly when I saw them load her into the ambulance."

Jenna nodded. "We're not here because we think you might have taken the baby. But you might have seen someone who could have been stalking my sister or who'd approached her about the baby."

Rome touched a hand to his chin. "Mostly, we have locals hanging out to visit and watch games. But we get strangers in here, too. Folks fly into Bozeman to get to Yellowstone. Some stay in town. Others rent cars and stay at resorts in West Yellowstone." He closed his eyes and pinched his nose. "People asked her all the time when she was due." He laughed. "I mean, you couldn't miss the fact she was gonna drop that baby any day. I only let her work behind the bar to offset her rent and make some tip money for groceries."

"Do you remember any of the people who asked about her baby or when she was due?" Cliff asked.

"Several guests asked. I can't recall anyone in

particular." His brow wrinkled. "She did talk with one of our regulars, Dave Waters. Nice guy. Always has a kind word for the staff and tips well. He and some of his friends come during football season to watch the games."

Jenna had hoped for more from the bar owner. The person who'd taken Brittany's baby could have been one of the people who'd shown an interest in her condition.

"Do you have video surveillance cameras on the bar?"

Rome shook his head. "I've been meaning to install a system; I just don't have the money to invest."

"Were you aware that my sister's apartment was ransacked since she left for the hospital?"

His eyes grew rounder. "This is the first I've heard. I was up early to go fishing with a friend. I never got any calls while I was out on the river." He pulled his cell phone out of his pocket, a frown creasing his brow. "What the hell? Eleven calls, and my phone never rang." He held up his cell phone to show them the number of calls he'd missed. "Why would someone trash her apartment? As far as I could tell, she had nothing to steal."

"Good question," Jenna said. "One we'd like to know the answer to."

"Wish I could help you." Martin shook his head.

"Can't believe someone took her baby. She must be beside herself."

"She is," Jenna said. "Think about it. If you remember anything that might help the case, call me." Jenna pulled a business card out of her wallet and handed it to the bar owner,

He stared down at the card, his eyes widening. He glanced up at Jenna. "FBI?"

Jenna's lips twisted. "Yeah, but I'm not officially on the case. I'm here because it's my sister and my niece."

The older man nodded. "Family."

"We've gathered all her belongings. I'll come back as soon as I can to clean," Jenna said. "Right now, I'm more worried about finding the baby."

"I'm sorry I'm not more help. Poor girl. She already had it rough. Let her know I'm thinking of her."

"I will," Jenna said. "She said nice things about you. Thank you for giving her a place to stay and earn some money."

The bar owner. "I figured she was young enough to be my daughter if I'd ever had one. I wouldn't want my daughter sleeping on the streets nine months pregnant."

"Like my sister told me, you're a good man, Mr. Martin." Jenna pushed out of the chair and stood, tossing a bill on the counter.

"Take your money," Martin said. "And take good

care of Brittany. She's high-spirited, but she works hard. She'll always have a job with me."

"Thank you." Jenna turned to Cliff. "I have to go to the bathroom, then I want to look at the other businesses around the bar and see if they have surveillance cameras."

Jenna left Cliff at the bar to finish his beer. She walked down the hallway to the door marked WOMEN and pushed through.

Inside, she hurried to a stall and quickly relieved her bladder. Once she was finished, she left the stall and washed her hands. As she reached for a paper towel from the dispenser, the bathroom door swung open behind her.

She turned to leave only to have her exit blocked by a man whose face was vaguely familiar.

"Oh," she said, startled to find a man in the women's bathroom. Her pulse quickened as she quickly assessed the situation and her options should the man attack her.

"You're in the wrong bathroom," she said, tossing the paper towel into the trash bin, freeing her hands in case she needed to defend herself or reach for the gun tucked beneath her jacket.

"You're Brittany's sister," the man said.

Jenna's eyes narrowed. "I am." She realized in that second who this guy was. "And you're Larry Sutton, the man who knocked her up." Her lips pressed together in a tight line.

"That's right. That baby is mine," he said. "And she ran off without telling me she was leaving or where she was going. I'm that baby's father. She had no right to take off with it."

"From what she told me, you weren't interested in the baby."

"I'm interested."

Jenna's eyes narrowed to slits. "And how do your wife and other children feel about that?"

"I don't know what you're talking about. I don't have a wife and children other than the one your sister was carrying. Where's the baby?" he demanded.

"That's the sixty-four-million-dollar question of the day." She lifted her chin. "By the way, the police are looking for you to ask that very question."

His brow lowered. "How would I know? Last night, I went to the hospital to see Brittany and the baby, but they wouldn't let me in."

"Why should they?" Jenna challenged. "Brittany said you wanted to put the child up for adoption."

"It was an option if she didn't want to keep the baby. But I want the baby. All she has to do is sign over her rights, and she can get on with her life."

Jenna shook her head. "Not happening. Brittany's keeping the baby. And since you're so intent on claiming your rights as the sperm donor, I'll make sure she takes you to court for child support."

His face turned a ruddy red. "This is between me and your sister. I suggest you butt out."

She lifted her chin, took a step forward and dropped her voice an octave. "Or what?"

"Where's Brittany?" he demanded. "I should be talking to her, not you."

"She's somewhere safe," Jenna said. "And she doesn't want anything to do with you."

"We'll see about that," he said. "That baby is mine. She can't take it away from me."

"You gave up any rights to her baby when you suggested putting it up for adoption and when you led her to believe you were single and available." Jenna met the man's gaze head-on. "Leave. My. Sister. And. Her. Baby. Alone."

"Or what?" He advanced on her, his fists clenched.

Jenna didn't back away. Instead, she braced herself to defend against any physical attack he might throw her way. "I'll make you wish you had."

The bathroom door pushed open.

"Jenna?" Cliff stepped through, frowning. The frown went feral when he spotted Larry. "What the hell? Jenna, are you okay?"

She nodded. "I'm fine. Please dial 911 and inform the police that one of their persons of interest in the baby's abduction is here."

Cliff glanced from Jenna to the man standing between them and nodded. He hit the numbers on his cell phone, his attention fixed on the man. "Yes, please inform Detective Schwope that Larry Sutton is in town at the Bear Claw Tavern."

"That's fine. Bring the cops." Larry crossed his arms over his chest. "I have nothing to hide. I think you and Brittany are the ones hiding something. *My* baby. And you're leading the authorities to believe it's been stolen."

The search for a Larry Sutton meeting his description in Salt Lake City had drawn a blank. The wife and children Brittany claimed he had hadn't surfaced. Then the man her sister walked out on showed up looking for the baby.

At that point, Jenna didn't know who to believe, though she leaned toward Brittany. One thing was certain. Whether or not he was lying about his marital status or his desire to keep his child, Larry Sutton didn't have the baby.

Why else would he corner Jenna, demanding to know where she was?

CHAPTER 10

JENNA LED the trio out of the women's bathroom, with Cliff bringing up the rear.

Cliff would be damned if he let the weasel of a baby daddy out of his sight. He almost wished the bastard would try to make a run for it. He'd take great pleasure in bringing him down.

They waited in awkward silence at a table in the barroom. Thankfully, Detective Schwope arrived five minutes later and took charge of Sutton.

After the hand-off, Cliff grabbed Jenna's hand. "Let's go."

She let him lead her out of the tavern to his truck before she ground to a halt. "Where are we going in such a hurry?"

"Back to the hospital." He opened the passenger door and waited for her to climb in.

"Why?" she asked as she adjusted her seatbelt.

"I want to look at video footage again. We have to have missed something. If Sutton said he tried to see Brittany last night, he should be on one of the videos. And if he's here demanding to know where the baby is, it means he doesn't have her."

Jenna nodded. "Unless he's an even better liar than we give him credit for. I don't think he's that smart."

Cliff rounded the truck and slid into the driver's seat. "There has to be someone else." He started the engine and shifted into Drive.

"I saw the janitor last night," Jenna said. "I didn't see his face, but I did note that he was tall with a thin build. Waters is the right height but has broader shoulders than the janitor I saw last night. Sutton is much shorter."

"Maybe that person is working for or with Waters or Sutton," Cliff suggested. "Or it's someone working alone. I just think we're chasing the wrong leads."

"It's too bad Sutton doesn't appear to have the baby." Her eyes narrowed. "I'd like to be the one to take him down."

Cliff grinned. "I was hoping he'd make a run for it. I wanted to grind him into the ground."

"My sister was convinced he has a wife and children in Salt Lake City. I know she's been a bit of a flake, but why would she lie?"

"Give Swede time. He'll get to the truth." Cliff

pulled out of the tavern parking lot onto the street, heading for the hospital.

They arrived at the hospital a few minutes later and parked.

Inside, Jenna flashed her FBI badge and asked to be escorted to the security office.

Jenna explained what she wanted to view and sat beside the security guard.

He brought up the video footage from the time Brittany had been brought into the hospital. They spent the next hour combing through the different camera angles, looking at the people entering the hospital and exiting after the baby had been delivered and moved to the nursery and, finally, to Brittany's room.

The janitor on the third floor arrived shortly after Brittany had delivered the baby.

"Let me look at the corridors leading to the back loading dock," Jenna said.

The guard brought up a couple of videos of two different hallways.

Jenna pointed to doors on either side of one of the hallways. "Where do these doors lead?"

The guard pointed to one. "That one goes to a storage closet. The other is the medical staff's locker rooms."

"Do all members of the medical staff use that room?" Jenna asked.

"Not all of them," the guard said. "Just the ones

who like to change out of their scrubs at the end of their shift."

He advanced the video at one and a half times the normal speed.

Nurse Grey entered the changing room, wearing her scrubs. Minutes later, she emerged carrying a large bag, the strap slung over her shoulder.

"Is it possible to see that room?" Jenna asked.

"Let me get a guard to escort you. I can't leave my station."

"While we wait," Jenna nodded toward the monitors, "let's look at the front entry where guests have to check in before being allowed to visit their family members."

The guard brought up the video of the front desk and ran it at an accelerated speed. As it neared a time shortly after Brittany delivered her baby, Jenna asked the guard to slow the rate.

A man wearing a hoodie stepped up to the desk.

"That's Sutton," Jenna said. "So, he was here at the hospital last night."

Cliff studied the image of the man they'd just encountered at the tavern. "He didn't have the baby today, or he wouldn't have cornered you looking for it."

Jenna's lips pursed. "And he's shorter than the janitor we saw on the third-floor video before it went dark."

Another security guard entered the room. "You needed an escort?" he asked.

The guard manning the video surveillance system nodded toward Jenna and Cliff. "Take these two to the medical staff's locker room."

"And we'd like to see the route from the elevators to the loading dock, if possible," Cliff added.

Jenna nodded.

"Take them where they need to go," the man in charge said.

"Yes, sir."

The guard led them through doors marked AUTHORIZED PERSONNEL ONLY and walked them to the back of the hospital through a maze of corridors. He paused at a service elevator.

"The janitor would've had to come out here with the cart," Jenna said.

The guard nodded and led them down the corridor, passing different doors. He unlocked them one by one for Jenna and Cliff to look inside at a supply room, mechanical hub, broom closet and the locker room.

Inside the last room was a wall of lockers, some with names taped to the door, a bathroom, a shower room and a laundry hamper for soiled scrubs.

Jenna ran her fingers across the locker marked Grey.

Cliff wondered what she was thinking.

They followed the guard out of the locker room.

Across the hall from the locker room was an open door leading into a room where a dozen rolling baskets were lined up against the wall. Some held scrubs, others were filled with sheets, another with blankets and still another with the baby blankets used to swaddle newborns.

"Nurse Grey was leaving about the time the baby went missing. She would've passed this door on her way out. Surely, she saw something."

"Wouldn't hurt to ask her again," Cliff said.

Jenna nodded.

They continued down the hallway to the door leading to the loading dock.

A man stood in a windowed office overlooking the dock. He stepped into the corridor as they approached.

"Is there someone in this office at all times?" Jenna asked.

The man shook his head. "We lock up after seven in the evening and open up again at four-thirty in the morning."

Jenna stared out the window to the loading dock. "Who has the keys to these doors?"

"It's a keycard system. Only a certain number of personnel can get in and out based on their employee ID."

"Like Robert Whitley?"

The man nodded. "A detective asked me about him earlier today. Whitley is on vacation this week.

He's somewhere on a guided fishing trip he's been planning for months."

"Do you know where?"

The man shook his head. "He told me, but I don't remember. I told the detective to check with his wife."

"How tall is Robert Whitley," Jenna asked.

The man grinned. "He's a couple of inches shorter than I am and heavier set."

Jenna frowned. "What are you, about five feet ten?"

"Five-nine on a good day," he said.

Jenna looked around a minute or two more, then glanced toward Cliff. "I've seen enough." She smiled at the dock worker. "Thank you."

The guard escorted them back to the hospital's front entrance, where Jenna flashed her FBI badge and asked for the addresses of Nurse Grey and Robert Whitley.

Cliff cupped Jenna's elbow and walked out of the hospital with her. "What are you thinking?"

"I want to see if Schwope followed up with Whitley's wife and asked where he left his hospital ID card. Then we need to pay Nurse Grey a visit."

Once in the truck, Cliff's stomach rumbled. He glanced at his watch. "It's getting late. You want to grab something to eat?"

"After we run by Nurse Grey's house." She handed the nurse's address to Cliff and then called

Detective Schwope, hitting the speaker button on her phone.

While Jenna's phone rang, Cliff entered Nurse Grey's address into the map application on his cell phone and shifted into drive.

"Special Agent Jenkins, you've got to be running on fumes by now."

She laughed. "I am. Did you check with Robert Whitley's wife about the location of his hospital ID card?"

"I did this afternoon. She said it was lying on his dresser in their bedroom where he'd left it before he went on his fishing trip."

"Has anyone been in her house since he's been gone?" Cliff asked, turning onto the main road

"She had a planning meeting yesterday with several volunteers who work at the food bank. I asked her to provide a list of names. She hasn't gotten back to me with that list. I'll let you know when she does."

"What about today?" Jenna asked.

"She said she's been gone most of the day at doctor's appointments."

"Anything interesting from your interview with Larry Sutton?"

"He claimed he arrived in town yesterday, an hour before the baby disappeared and went straight to the hospital where he was told he couldn't see Brittany. From there, he went to a hotel across town and got a room. I checked with the hotel. They verified he was there at the exact time the baby disappeared."

Jenna sighed. "Did you ask him about his wife and kids in Salt Lake City?"

"I did. He said he was single and didn't know what I was talking about."

Jenna snorted. "That's what I got out of him. He seems very interested in the baby. It doesn't add up with what Brittany said about him wanting to put it up for adoption."

"Do you trust that what your sister is telling you is the truth?" the detective asked.

"Brittany has always been rebellious and marched to the beat of her own drum, but she's never lied to me. She owns up to her mistakes."

"I had to ask," Schwope said, "since her story isn't matching Sutton's."

"I understand. Thanks." She ended the call and laid the cell phone in her lap.

Cliff shot a glance in Jenna's direction. "Do you think Sutton is telling the truth?"

"If he is, that would mean that Brittany is lying." She shook her head. "I'd believe my sister over Sutton any day."

"Are you too close to this case to be unbiased?" Cliff asked.

"Maybe." She lifted her phone and dialed another number, again placing the phone on speaker so Cliff could hear the conversation.

Following the directions on the map, he turned left at the next street.

"Special Agent Jenkins." Hank Patterson's voice filled the truck cab. "Have you found the baby?"

"Sadly, no," she said. "Is Brittany close? I want to ask her some questions."

"Hold on, I'll find her. She and Sadie are in the living room with the kids. It's just up the stairs." A moment later, he said, "Here's Brittany."

"Jenna?" Brittany's voice came over the receiver. "Have you found her?"

"Hey, Britt." Jenna's gaze met Cliff's, her lips pressing together. "No, sweetie. Not yet."

Brittany sighed. "I know you're trying. It's just so hard to be here and not close to you."

"I feel the same, but I'm glad you're safe. We went by your apartment and packed your things."

"Thank you. And thank you for the clothes you sent. I'll return them when I can."

"No hurry. I found a brochure among your papers for a Little Angel Adoption Agency. I thought you didn't want to go through an agency and had agreed to Mr. Waters because it was more personal."

"That brochure was something Larry brought to me, insisting I use them to place our baby for adoption. I thought I'd thrown it away. I couldn't place my baby with an agency. How could I be certain she would go to a good home? But Larry was so insistent that I wasn't ready to be a parent and that keeping the baby would ruin my life."

"Speaking of Larry," Jenna said, "he showed up at the tavern, said you'd run away with his baby and he wanted to keep it."

"Oooo, that bast—" Brittany stopped mid-curse. "Sorry, there are little ears here. Larry is a master manipulator. He makes you feel like everything he says is the truth, and any opposing opinion is dumb. That's why I stayed with him so long. He was the hotshot pharmaceutical salesman driving a sports car. I barely got out of high school with a diploma. Don't trust him. Once I left him, I realized he'd been feeding me lies from day one."

"You say he has a wife and children in Salt Lake City. He flat-out denies it. How do you know this? We can't find a Larry Sutton fitting his description in Salt Lake City."

"Again, he's a master manipulator. I wouldn't be surprised if Larry Sutton isn't even his name. I caught him on a video call, wishing his wife a happy anniversary. He thought I was asleep." She snorted. "They were celebrating ten years together. The children all got on the video call. A boy and a girl. They called him Daddy and asked when he was coming home. He said he'd be back in Salt Lake City at the end of the week. I asked him who he'd been talking to, hoping he would confess. He said it was a work colleague. I called him out on the fact those *colleagues* referred to him as Daddy and Darling."

"Why didn't you leave him then?" Jenna asked.

"He told me he was in the process of filing for a divorce and didn't want them to know yet. But that was months ago. I was stupid to believe him," Brittany said. "You're smarter than I am. Don't believe anything he says. I don't know why he told you he wanted our baby. He was adamant about putting her up for adoption with that agency."

"Thanks for clarifying," Jenna said. "Are you feeling okay?"

Her sister sighed. "As well as can be expected. Sadie and Hank are terrific hosts, and their children are adorable. I'm just anxious to get my baby back. I hope she's okay. She's too little for this to happen to her. I hope whoever has her is taking good care of her."

"Me, too," Jenna said, her heart pinching hard in her chest at the thought of that tiny baby with the soft orange fuzz across the top of her head. "We're working hard to find her."

"I know you are. I love you for it," Brittany said.

"I have to go now. Take care of yourself, sweetie. I'll see you soon. Can you hand the phone back to Hank?"

A moment later, Hank said, "I have Swede checking on the Little Angel Adoption Agency. At first blush, he says it appears legitimate. They even have good reviews on the internet. He's digging deeper."

"Any hits on the facial recognition of the photo we sent?" Cliff asked as he slowed for a traffic light.

"Swede's running that now. There were fifty potential hits scattered across Montana, Wyoming, Utah, and North and South Dakota. He's working on narrowing it down to a handful. Have you made any headway in Bozeman?"

"We met with David Waters," Cliff said. "He's the man Brittany had agreed to let adopt her baby before she changed her mind."

"Any chance he has the baby?" Hank asked.

Jenna shook her head. "He appeared just as concerned about the baby's disappearance and genuinely upset. He also has an alibi, and his shoulders are too broad to match the janitor's build."

"Could the coveralls the janitor wore be misleading?" Hank asked. "Could Waters' concern be an act?"

"Maybe," Jenna said.

"Swede's also looking into Waters' background," Hank said. "We have a lot of feelers out. It's only a matter of time before information flows in."

"We just informed Brittany that Larry Sutton is in Bozeman," Jenna said. "He confronted me, looking for *his* baby."

"If he's looking for it," Hank said, "that means he doesn't have it, right?"

"That's what we think," Cliff said. "Which brings us back to the big question. Who has the baby?"

"No leads on the janitor?" Hank asked.

"The ID card used was from a maintenance man who is on a fishing vacation all this week," Cliff said.

"Can anyone verify his location?"

"He's off the grid, according to his wife," Cliff said.

"From how others describe him, he doesn't fit the description of the janitor I saw in the hallway," Jenna said. "Whitley is short and stout. The man I saw in the maintenance uniform was tall and slim."

"Something's gotta break soon," Hank said.

"I hope so. That baby needs to be in a safe and stable environment," Jenna said. "With her mother."

"Agreed," Hank said. "What's your next move?"

"We're headed to Nurse Grey's house. The surveillance footage shows her exiting the medical staff's locker room across the hall from the laundry staging area. She met with the detective this morning when she came on her shift. She said she didn't see anyone out of the ordinary on the labor and delivery floor. The detective didn't ask if she'd seen anyone in the hallway outside the locker room.

"She could've passed the janitor pushing the cart at some point," Jenna continued. "She seems the friendly type. She might even have said hello and looked at the man's face."

"Good luck," Hank said. "Swede's still

searching for more information regarding Larry Sutton and David Waters. We'll let you know what we find."

Cliff pulled up to a small cottage at the end of a street lined with older houses, some with overgrown yards and peeling paint.

A light glowed through a curtain in the front picture window. An older model sedan was parked in the gravel driveway.

Jenna stared at the house as she unbuckled her seatbelt. "I overheard Nurse Grey talking to another nurse about her mother's memory issues. I'm not sure, but I think her mother lives with her." She slid out of her seat onto the ground.

Cliff dropped down from the driver's side and met Jenna in front of the truck.

"I hope we're not dropping in too late." She checked her watch.

"Most people don't go to bed this early," Cliff noted.

Jenna marched up the porch steps and knocked lightly on the door.

Cliff could hear a voice inside.

"Do you hear that?" Jenna leaned her ear against the door panel. "Someone is singing."

Cliff lifted his chin toward the door. "Knock again."

When Jenna tapped a little harder, the door edged open slightly.

The singing stopped for a moment and then started again.

"Nurse Grey," Jenna called out through the gap. "It's Jenna Jenkins, Brittany Berry's sister. We'd like to talk to you."

The singing stopped.

A chill that had nothing to do with the cool night air slithered across Cliff's skin.

He started to reach for the door handle, but Jenna's hand caught his wrist before his fingers touched the knob.

She reached her hand beneath her jacket and pulled out her Glock.

Now, that chill snaked down Cliff's spine.

"Nurse Grey, it's Jenna Jenkins, FBI. I'm coming in for a wellness check." She nudged the door open with her elbow and stood back as it swung inward and light spilled out onto the porch.

Cliff peered into the small entryway.

The singing started again, along with a creaking sound like that of a rocking chair.

"Hush, little baby, don't say a word," the voice sang in a voice that cracked with age.

Jenna stepped through the door, her handgun braced in both hands.

Cliff entered behind her, his own gun drawn and at the ready.

As they cleared the walls of the entryway, the living room stretched to their left with an overstuffed floral sofa and a rocking recliner with its back to them.

The recliner rocked, the springs creaking each time.

A gray tuft of hair stuck up over the back of the recliner.

Jenna entered the living room. "Nurse Grey?"

The gray-haired person in the rocking recliner continued singing. "Mama's gonna buy you a mockingbird."

Cliff walked around the recliner to find an old woman holding what appeared to be a baby blanket in her arms.

"If that mockingbird won't sing," the woman sang, her voice cracking.

"Excuse me, ma'am," Cliff said. "Is Nurse Grey here?"

The old woman stopped singing and stared up at Cliff. "Are you here to fix the stove?"

Cliff smiled at the woman. "No, ma'am. I'm here to see your daughter."

She blinked up at him. "My daughter?"

"Yes, ma'am. Your daughter," Cliff said. "Do you know where she is?"

"She's in the nursery, of course." The old woman pushed her feet against the floor, setting the rocker in motion again, and sang, "I'm gonna buy you a diamond ring."

"Jesus Christ," Jenna's voice sounded from another room. "Cliff."

The urgency in her tone made Cliff hurry out of the living room and down a short hallway to a room two doors down.

Jenna stood in the open doorway, her face pale in the light of the single bulb hanging in the hallway. "I found Nurse Grey," she said softly.

Cliff stepped up beside Jenna and stared down at the lifeless body of Nurse Grey.

CHAPTER 11

Jenna bent to feel for a pulse, knowing she wouldn't find one.

The nurse's face was pale, her eyes opened wide, her expression frozen in a soundless scream.

Straightening, Jenna glanced around what appeared to be a bedroom with an old-fashioned, white iron bed covered with a hand-sewn quilt.

In the middle of the bed was a laundry basket, a short stack of what appeared to be disposable diapers and a canister of baby formula.

Jenna's heart skipped several beats as she hurried toward the laundry basket.

Inside the basket was a folded baby blanket like the ones they'd wrapped Blakely in at the hospital. And nothing else.

No baby.

Jenna looked around the small room, checking in

drawers, under the bed and in the closet. Still...no baby.

She expanded her search to include every inch of the house. Cliff followed, with his gun held out in front of him.

Jenna holstered hers, more concerned about finding the baby than her own safety.

She finally came to a stop with Nurse Grey at her feet. "She was here. My sister's baby was here."

The sound of singing drifted in from the living room. "Hush, little baby, don't say a word..." Then humming sounded.

Jenna pulled her cell phone out of her pocket and called the detective.

Detective Schwope answered on the first ring. "Special Agent Jenkins, you're working late."

"I'm at Lena Grey's house. She's dead."

"The baby?"

"No." Jenna's stomach knotted. "Nurse Grey is dead. Based on bruising around her throat, I'd guess she was strangled."

"Jesus," the detective said.

"I think my sister's baby was here. Unfortunately, she's not here now."

"Any idea who might have done it?" the detective asked.

"None. But whoever killed Nurse Grey has the baby."

"I'll send the crime scene investigators."

"We'll need someone from social services as well to place Nurse Grey's mother in a memory care facility."

Cliff waited with Jenna until the police arrived and took over.

Back in the truck after what felt like a very long time, he turned to Jenna. "We're getting a bite to eat, and then we're calling it a night."

Jenna frowned. "But—"

He held up a hand. "We haven't eaten all day, your dog needs to go outside, we have no new leads and we're running on fumes. We'll get some rest and start fresh in the morning." He shifted into drive and left the little cottage, driving back toward Jenna's home.

"I feel like I should continue to search until we find her. She's a helpless infant, being jerked around by people who don't have her best interests at heart. If they're not careful, she could die."

"And I'm telling you, your brain suffers when you go without sleep for too long," Cliff said. "Get at least five hours of sleep and see how much that helps your thought processes."

Jenna sighed. "Might as well. We've run out of options. The only person who might have seen the fake janitor's face is now dead." Her brow wrinkled. "What I don't understand is why Nurse Grey had the baby here and didn't tell anyone."

Cliff stared at the road in front of him. "She must

have carried her out in that oversized bag we saw in the video."

"I don't think she had that bag on the third floor." Jenna glanced at Cliff. "Could it have been a two-man operation?"

Cliff shrugged. "Maybe."

Jenna pressed a hand to her belly. "Turn right at the next road."

He turned right and increased his speed.

"At the next light, turn left and pull into the parking lot."

Cliff's brow knotted. "Where are you taking us?"

"You'll see." Her stomach rumbled loudly.

Cliff shook his head. "We shouldn't have gone so long without stopping for something to eat and drink."

Jenna's lips tightened. "We had more important things to do."

"Well, you can't function without sleep or fuel to power your body." As he pulled into the parking lot, a slow smile spread across his face. "Okay, this will address the fuel to power your body."

"It's the best barbecue in the city." Jenna pushed the door open. "We can get it to go and take it back to my place. I need to check on Brutus. My neighbor takes care of him when I'm late getting home, but I know he likes it when I come home."

They ordered a pound each of sliced brisket and pulled pork, potato salad and baked beans. Once the

ELLE JAMES

food was packaged for carryout, Cliff carried it out to the truck.

The scent of warm barbecue filled the cab's interior, making Jenna's stomach rumble loudly.

By the time they arrived at her house, she was so hungry she couldn't think straight.

She unlocked the door and bent to scratch Brutus behind the ears. "Hey, big guy." He leaned into her and stared at Cliff, keeping a close eye on him.

"Where do you want this?" he said, carrying the bag of food into her little house.

"On the table in the kitchen," she said. "I'm going to let Brutus out before I eat. Don't wait on me."

Jenna walked through the kitchen to the back door and twisted the deadbolt. All she had to do was crack the door a little and Brutus darted out into the fenced back yard.

She stepped out onto the porch and drew in a deep breath of clear, Montana air.

Cliff stepped out onto the porch behind her, close enough to touch her, though he didn't. "It's amazing that no matter how awful your day is, a clear, star-filled night reminds you how beautiful life can be." He spoke softly, his breath warm against the back of her neck.

"It is beautiful," she said.

"Absolutely beautiful," he murmured, his voice low.

Knowing he was directly behind her, Jenna

184

turned to face him and laid her hands against his broad chest. She liked how warm and solid he was. A rock she could hold onto when the current was too strong. She'd always stood on her own two feet, never relying on someone else to protect her. Having the Navy SEAL at her side didn't diminish her own strength but reinforced it and made her stronger.

"Thanks for being with me today," she said. "This case means so very much to me, I'm glad I have an extra pair of eyes to see what I'm seeing and another mind to sift through the clues."

Starlight turned Cliff's dark hair an inky blue.

He wrapped his arms around her, pulling her close. "You're an amazing woman, Special Agent Jenkins. I can't think of any place I'd rather be at this moment. And I'd really like to kiss you."

She smiled up at him. "Are you intimidated because I'm wearing a gun?"

He grinned. "No. I think it's kind of sexy. I've never dated a woman who carries a gun everywhere. It's nice to know you can take care of yourself when I'm not around." He tilted his head. "Are you intimidated because *I* carry a gun?"

Jenna tilted her head to one side. "Actually, I'm more intimidated by how attractive I find you."

He cupped her cheek and brushed his thumb across her lips. "Attraction isn't a good thing?"

She leaned her face into his palm. "No. I'm not good at relationships. I'm not good at showing affection, and I think I'm boring in bed." A weak smile played at the corners of her lips. "How's that for oversharing on a first date? Not that we're on a first date, and now, we never will go on a date because I'm weird and don't know when to shut up." With a sigh, she pressed her lips to his palm. "I guess what I'm trying to say is that I like having you around. I never realized how solitary my job could be until you followed me for the past twenty-four hours."

"Running into you in the stairwell has been a game-changer for me. I avoided commitment for a long time. I thought it was because of the job." He bent and touched his lips to hers. "I was wrong," he whispered. "It wasn't the job. I think it was the girl."

Jenna's pulse quickened, and her fingers curled into his shirt. "This attraction…doesn't have to mean anything permanent. I'm okay with that. In fact, I'm used to it. If something…happens between us, you can move on after a night, a week or whatever. I'll understand. It wouldn't be the first time."

Cliff claimed her mouth, stopping her from uttering more inane and self-deprecating comments. Why was she so confident in her work as an FBI agent and pathetic with personal relationships?

She didn't know. And with Cliff's lips on her mouth, she didn't care. As long as he kept kissing her, she didn't have to think about anything else.

Her hands climbed up his chest and encircled his neck, pulling him closer.

Cliff reached behind him and opened the door.

He bent, scooped her up in his arms and carried her across the threshold without breaking the kiss.

Once through the door, he kicked it shut and brought his head up. "What do you want, Jenna?" he asked. "A night, a week, a lifetime?"

Held in his arms as though she weighed nothing, she stared up into his eyes. "We have tonight," she whispered. "Let's get to know each other. If it goes further, we can renegotiate."

"Sounds so businesslike," Cliff chuckled.

She laughed, feeling joy for the first time since the baby went missing, maybe for the first time ever. "I feel anything but businesslike with you holding me in your arms."

"Good." He grinned. "Because business is the last thing on my mind."

She looked up at him with a teasing smile. "I thought you were hungry."

"I am." His mouth brushed hers. "For you."

"What about dinner?"

"Do you want to eat now?" he asked, his body tense against hers. "We can."

"I can wait." She shook her head slowly, though her heartbeat raced like a grass fire, sweeping through her with molten blood. "Are we going to do this?"

"Completely up to you," he said, eyebrows rising. "You want to kiss and be done. We can do it." He tipped his head slightly and grimaced. "It'll be hard to apply the brakes, but I'll respect your wishes."

After the drama of the past twenty-four hours and the uncertainties outstanding with the case, Jenna felt positive about one thing—her need for this man, this stranger.

She pointed to the hallway. "My bedroom. Now. Dinner can wait." Then she cupped his cheek and met his gaze. "I want the full Monty. No brakes."

Cliff laughed out loud, making Brutus bark. Then he kissed her hard and carried her into her bedroom, kicking the door closed behind him, leaving Brutus on the other side.

He stopped beside the bed and lowered her legs until her feet touched the ground.

With him in her bedroom, his shoulders so broad they filled the space, Jenna hesitated. "Is it wrong to want this so badly?" She laid a hand on his chest. "We only just met." Her fingers gripped the opening of his leather jacket and spread it wide and over his shoulders. It slid off his back and arms and dropped to the floor.

"Some people," he said as he divested her of her jacket, "feel an instant connection. I felt that with you."

She chuckled as she loosened the buckle on his shoulder holster. "You felt the connection when you plowed into me in the stairwell?"

He nodded. "And you?" He removed her shoulder holster and laid it gently on a nearby chair.

"I had no choice but to feel that connection when a gorgeous man hit me like a linebacker and landed on top of me." She slid the leather straps off his shoulders and deposited his holster and gun on the same chair as his. "Seriously, I think it was the first time you kissed my forehead. You didn't think about it. You just did it."

"You could've slapped my face into tomorrow."

"Anyone else, I probably would have. But with you..." she stared up into his eyes, her brow twisting, "it felt gentle. Natural. Right." She leaned up on her toes and pressed her mouth to his in a tentative kiss.

At first, he let her take the lead. When she traced the seam of his mouth, he opened, and she thrust her tongue inside.

As the kiss deepened, their arms tightened around each other. Her hands smoothed over his arms, and she reveled in their thick, muscular strength. Her breasts pressed against the hardness of his chest, and suddenly, she couldn't get close enough.

Jenna broke the kiss and stepped away.

Cliff's arms fell to his sides, and a frown pulled at his brow.

Her lips tipped upward as she reached for the hem of her shirt and dragged it up and over her head.

Taking his cue from her, Cliff tore his shirt over his head and tossed it aside. Then, it became a race to remove all their clothes until they stood in front of each other, naked and breathing fast.

Jenna's heart pounded wildly against her ribs. She should feel self-conscious about baring her body before a man she'd know only a day, but she didn't.

The fire in his eyes and the way his gaze swept over her gave her courage and made her feel beautiful.

As she drank him in, her gaze sweeping him from head to toe, Jenna's breath caught and held; heat coiled at her core, and fire burned in her veins.

Cliff reached out and captured her face in his hands, bringing his lips to hover over hers. "You're so very beautiful."

"You're not so bad yourself," she whispered against his lips.

He brushed his mouth across hers, then slid his lips down the long column of her throat, stopping to press a kiss to the pulse thumping at the base. His hands rose to capture her breasts, lifting them as if weighing them in his palms. Then he bent to take one distended nipple into his mouth, where he teased it with his tongue, rolled it between his teeth and sucked on it until her back arched and her knees grew weak.

His hands slid around to her back, cupped her ass and lifted her, settling her onto the side of the bed. Nudging her knees apart, he stepped between her legs, laced his fingers behind her head and bent to capture her mouth in an earthshattering kiss laying her back against the comforter.

His mouth blazed a path down her neck and over her collarbone to pause at one breast, where he flicked and teased until the nipple puckered into a tight little bead. He moved to the other and treated it to the same while his hand slid over her flat belly, angling down to the juncture of her thighs.

Jenna ran her fingers along his back, tracing the scars she could feel, her fingers massaging taut skin stretched over hard muscles.

Cliff moved lower, his mouth skimming over her torso, his fingers slipping between her folds. He dipped a digit into her wet channel and came back to touch her there, swirling and flicking until her back arched, and she moaned.

He parted her folds with his thumbs and leaned in, touching her clit with the tip of his tongue.

The spark of sensation raced through her, so intense Jenna gasped.

Cliff stopped what he was doing. "Did I hurt you?"

"Oh, sweet heaven," she cried. "Don't stop!"

He chuckled and touched her again with his tongue, flicking her gently, swirling around that sensitive nubbin until Jenna writhed beneath him.

The tension built, rising quickly until Jenna burst over the edge into the most incredible orgasm she'd ever experienced. Wave after wave of release washed through her, shooting from her core outward to the tips of her fingers.

He worked her until the very last tremor. She fell back against the comforter, spent, sated but wanting more.

Once she'd caught her breath, Jenna gripped his arms and tugged. "That was great, but I want more."

He rose from where he'd knelt on the floor, grabbed his jeans and dug a condom out of his wallet.

When Jenna started to scoot back on the bed, he hooked an arm beneath one of her knees and shook his head. "Not yet. There's more than one position." He rolled the condom over his thick shaft. "I want to explore all of them."

Her heart thundered, and the heat that had ebbed flared into a whole new flame.

He pressed his cock to her entrance, dipped into her slick channel a little, then pulled out. The next dip went deeper. He pulled out.

On fire and beyond patience, Jenna wrapped her legs around his waist. When he dipped again, she dug her heels into his buttocks and brought him all the way home.

He felt so good inside her, filling her so completely, she couldn't tell where he ended and she began. After a long, still moment, he pulled out, hooked his arms beneath her knees and rocked in and out of her, increasing the speed of his thrusts until he pumped like a piston, hard and fast.

Just when she thought he would come, he pulled free.

The sudden absence made her breath hitch.

As quickly as he'd left her, he reached for her, flipped her onto her belly and slid into her from behind.

Jenna's fingers curled into the comforter as he rode her hard, the angle of his approach causing new sensations to explode inside.

His body tensed behind her, the hands gripping her hips tightened, and he pulled free.

"Gah!" she cried. "You're such a damned tease."

He laughed, flipped her onto her back, scooted her up onto the mattress and lay between her legs, slipping his shaft into her in a slow, sensual glide until he was fully seated, his balls warm against her ass. He pulled out as slowly as he'd entered and paused.

"This makes three," he said and kissed her, thrusting his tongue into her mouth at the same time he thrust his cock deep into her.

Jenna grasped his hips, her fingers digging into the flesh of his tight ass.

Her own body responded to the friction, her core coiling tighter with each thrust.

He slipped in and out of her, moving faster, his muscles tensing until he plunged into her one last time.

Jenna's second release came in unison with Cliff's,

her body trembling, his cock pulsing.

They seemed frozen in that position, milking their orgasms to the very last tremor.

Jenna lay back against the mattress, her body spent, her muscles weak and shaky.

Cliff dropped down on her, his weight crushing the air from her lungs.

She didn't care. If she died at that moment, she'd die knowing blissful satisfaction like none she'd felt before.

Cliff pulled free of her and rolled to the side, bringing her to rest her head in the crook of his arm.

"I have no words," she said, her voice ragged as if she'd run a marathon.

"I do have one," he grinned. "Wow."

They lay for several minutes without speaking, gathering the shreds of their strength.

Finally, Cliff pushed up onto one elbow and stared down at her. "I'd like to negotiate more than one night."

She laughed. "I believe an agreement can be achieved. But I don't like to make deals on an empty stomach."

"Then let's feed the beast," he said and smacked her bare bottom. Cliff rolled out of the bed and held out a hand for her.

She grasped it and let him pull her to her feet and into his arms. "Mmm. I like the way you feel skin-to-skin."

He nuzzled her neck. "Same." His hard cock nudged her belly. "We can continue this train of thought after dinner."

Cliff swept his clothes off the floor, tossed his shirt toward her and pulled on his jeans.

Dressed in Cliff's shirt that hung down to mid-thigh, Jenna padded barefooted into the kitchen.

Brutus danced around her, eager for some affection and food.

While she fed the dog, Cliff laid out the barbecue.

They ate, talking about dogs, their childhoods and anything but the case. When they were done, they straightened the kitchen, put away the food and sent Brutus out for one more potty break.

When they came back inside, they raced for the bedroom and fell, laughing onto her bed, and made love again.

Exhausted, they lay in each other's arms.

Jenna's thoughts drifted back to Baby Blakely. "We're missing something," she whispered.

He didn't ask her what she was talking about. "Yes, we are."

"I get the feeling the clue we're looking for has to do with the employee ID. Someone took it from Whitley's house and put it back." Jenna sat up in the bed and reached for her phone.

"Who are you calling?"

"Detective Schwope."

"It's getting late," Cliff said.

195

Jenna glanced at the clock. "It's only nine. He'll be awake."

Before she could call the number, her phone rang in her hand. Hank Patterson's caller ID appeared on the screen.

"This is Jenna," she answered.

"Hank here. I have Swede on speaker. He's found some interesting information you need to know."

Her gut clenched as she put her phone on speaker. "Shoot."

CHAPTER 12

"HEY, SPECIAL AGENT JENKINS. SWEDE HERE." Hank's computer guru's voice was deep and decisive, with an underlying gentleness that made Cliff feel confident the man had people's best interests at heart.

"Using the databases you suggested, we combed through the facial recognition hits and found a few guys matching Larry's photo." Swede drew in a breath and let it out on a sigh. "Of course, there's Larry Sutton in Billings, Montana. There's also Lawrence Sanders in Fargo, North Dakota. Leonard Sweeney in Salt Lake City has been married to Darlene Sweeney for nine years, and they have two children based on their income tax returns and public birth records."

"The asshole has a girl in every port," Cliff said.

"Exactly," Hank said. "The Montana and North Dakota Larrys don't have much to go on besides the driver's licenses and addresses. Swede found your sister's name linked to the post office address system in Billings. A Sandra Neal is linked to the address in Fargo. And, get this, Sandra Neal recently had a baby and gave it up for adoption, with Lawrence Sanders signing off on the birth certificate as the father."

"Let me guess," Jenna met Cliff's gaze. "The adoption agency is Little Angels."

"Bingo," Swede said. "I tapped into Lawrence Sanders's credit report, which isn't good. He has maxed out three high-dollar credit cards, the largest charges incurred in Las Vegas casinos. He owes over fifty thousand dollars."

Jenna whistled. "He's an adulterer, con artist and a gambler." She shook her head. "My sister was smart to leave the jerk."

"It gets even more interesting," Hank said. "He had a large deposit made to his bank in Fargo from a corporation called LACube out of a bank based in Grand Cayman."

"LACube?" Jenna frowned.

"As in LAAA?" Cliff asked.

"That would be our guess," Hank said. "Little Angels Adoption Agency."

Jenna's eyes rounded, and her face lost all color. "He's selling babies to the adoption agency? Bastard. Oh, sweet Jesus. Larry wants Brittany's baby so he can sell her." She punched the comforter. "And he almost had her convinced."

Cliff wrapped an arm around Jenna. "He has to be the one who now has Baby Blakely."

"Why did he have to kill Nurse Grey? And who else is involved in smuggling the baby out of the hospital? It had to be the man in the jumpsuit. A man we have yet to identify," Jenna sighed. "If Larry has the baby, we need to catch him before he transfers her to the agency, and God knows what family willing to foot the bill."

Hank continued, "His phone shows his location at a motel about a mile from where you're staying in Bozeman. Swede was able to tap into his cell phone tracking application after we talked to you earlier. We've been tracking him since. Your sister says he won't go anywhere without his cell phone. He's been back to the tavern and driven around Jenna's address some this evening, even stopping for a while down the street from your house. Eventually, he returned to the motel."

Jenna's eyes narrowed. "Then again, if Larry's still hanging around—"

"—he doesn't have what he came for," Cliff finished.

"The baby," Hank said.

"And we're back to the mystery janitor." Jenna drummed her fingers on the comforter.

"I did some digging into David and Trudy Waters. David was a graduate of Baylor University in Texas. He met his wife there. They married after they grad-

ELLE JAMES

uated. She's had a number of miscarriages and one live birth. The baby died of SIDS at four months old."

"David Waters told her all that."

"I did a fact check to make sure he wasn't lying," Swede said. "He was telling the truth. When we searched for Trudy's maiden name, I learned she was Trudy Duvall, daughter of Thomas and Ruth Duvall."

"Of Duvall Industries?" Jenna asked. "The oil and real estate magnet?"

"That's the one," Swede confirmed. "Trudy was a Dallas Debutant on her way to becoming one of the most eligible bachelorettes in the state. She participated in all the debutant functions and went to all the right social events. And then nothing."

"What do you mean *nothing*?" Jenna asked.

"She disappeared before her senior year in the college preparatory high school she attended."

"How can someone as high-profile as that disappear?" Jenna held up a hand. "Never mind. I already know. Money can make a lot of things disappear."

"The sleazier tabloids rumored she was pregnant and hiding away to have the baby since she was out of sight for a full year."

Cliff leaned toward the phone, caught up in the story of a woman he'd never met. "Was she pregnant?"

"I didn't find any medical records proving she was with child. However, I dug into Thomas Duvall's personal tax records. He donated fifty thousand dollars to an organization that works with young, single pregnant women, helping them make choices. They provide counseling and access to medical care for mothers carrying their babies to term and keeping them or giving them up for adoption. They also counsel women on the option of abortion."

"Poor kid," Jenna said. "All of those choices would be difficult."

"In that same year, Duvall paid monthly payments to a Mental Health Rehabilitation Facility in Missoula, Montana."

"They sent her that far away from home?" Jenna's heart hurt for the teen who'd had to give up a baby.

"I'm sending you a photo of Trudy Duvall the spring before she disappeared," Swede said.

Jenna's phone pinged with an incoming text. She opened the text and enlarged the photo. It was a photo of a young woman in a white gown, standing alone, with another photograph of a dozen young women in white dresses.

"The woman standing beside the group picture is Trudy Duvall," Swede said. "She's also in the group photo at the center back."

Trudy stood in the center back because she was the tallest, standing several inches taller than the girls on either side of her. Her features were a little on the plain side, and she wore a slim-fitting dress that clung to her lithe, athletic build, emphasizing her model-slim hips and small breasts.

"This photo was taken during her junior year of high school," Swede said.

"If she disappeared because she was pregnant and now is having difficulties having a baby, she could be feeling desperate," Jenna mused. "Hank, Swede, thank you for the information. I need to check on something," she said. "Please say hello to my sister for me."

"Will do," Hank said.

Jenna ended the call and placed another, putting it on speaker.

"Special Agent Jenkins, do you ever sleep?" Detective Schwope asked.

"Did you get the names of the people who came to Whitley's house for the food bank meeting?"

"I did. She sent them about an hour ago."

"Can you share that list with me?" Jenna asked, a buzz of adrenaline building inside.

"Looking for someone in particular?" Schwope asked. "Sending a photo of Mrs. Whitley's handwritten list."

Jenna clicked on the photo, enlarged it and skimmed through the names.

Second from the bottom was Trudy Waters.

Jenna's heart beat faster.

"Jenkins, you still with me?" Schwope asked.

"I am," she said as she swung her legs off the bed and grabbed her jeans. "All this time, we've been looking for a male janitor. What if the fake janitor was a female?"

"You got one in mind?" Schwope asked.

"Trudy Waters' house," she said. "I'm heading over there now."

"I'll get a police unit headed that way."

"If Trudy has the baby, it's highly likely she's mentally unstable." Jenna threw her T-shirt over her head and shot a glance toward Cliff.

Fully dressed in his jeans, T-shirt and boots, Cliff slung his shoulder holster over his shoulders and handed Jenna hers.

Grabbing their jackets, they ran for the door. Brutus barked and ran after them.

"Sorry, dude," she said. With a more forceful tone and a stern look, she said, "Stay."

The dog immediately sat back on his haunches and stared at Jenna.

"Good dog," Cliff said.

Jenna held the door open.

Cliff darted through and ran for his truck while Jenna closed and locked the door.

He had the truck engine revved and the shift in reverse by the time Jenna hopped into the passenger seat.

Seconds later, they were speeding through town, heading for the edge of town where a newer subdivision had estates with one to five-acre lots. The Waters' home was the furthest west, with a view of the mountains silhouetted by starlight in the distance.

As they neared the home, Cliff turned off the headlights and slowed to a stop well before arriving at the driveway. He parked in front of the home before the one they were aiming for, killed the engine and dropped down from his seat.

Jenna met him in front of the truck. As she stepped out, he grabbed her arm and swung her around, pulling her into a quick embrace.

"I just want you to know, I think you're beautiful, smart, strong and sexy as hell. Some say when you know, you know. I know. When this is all said and done, I'm negotiating for the full Monty." He claimed her lips in a quick, hard kiss. "I'm pretty sure I'm in love with you, Jenkins."

When he released her, she hesitated, staring up into his eyes. "Are you serious?"

"Never more serious in my life."

A smile blossomed across her face. "You picked a helluva time to tell me."

He shrugged. "It felt natural."

She leaned up on her toes and kissed him. "Although something can be said about timing, I think we can come to a mutually satisfying agreement." She held a finger up. "Hold that thought."

He caught the finger. "I'm holding it. Now, go get 'em. I've got your six."

She spun and jogged toward the Waters' house. Cliff kept pace close behind her.

They swung wide to approach from the side, out

of range of the huge picture windows that were all dark. No lights shone in the front rooms or in any of the second-story windows on the front of the house.

Jenna rounded to the back of the house. A light shone through a window from what appeared to be the kitchen. Another light glowed in a second-story window above.

Jenna tiptoed up the steps of a wide, wraparound porch and approached the door to the kitchen. She pulled the gun from her holster with one hand, reached for the doorknob with the other and twisted it gently.

Expecting it to be locked, she was surprised when the knob turned easily in her hand. She pushed open the door and peered inside.

The large kitchen, with its huge gas stove, smooth quartz countertops and a commercial-size refrigerator, was a gourmet cook's dream. For the most part, it was neat and clean, except for the drawer hanging with a collection of knives scattered across the counter.

Jenna rounded a large island on one end while Cliff came around the other side and tripped, nearly landing on his face.

The obstacle that had nearly sent him sailing moved and moaned.

Jenna shone a flashlight toward the floor.

Holy hell, it was a man lying against the cabinet doors, his wrists and ankles secured with zip ties and a strip of duct tape sealing his mouth shut. A dark bruise swelled above his temple.

Cliff dropped to his haunches and pulled the tape from the man's mouth.

Jenna knelt beside the man. "Mr. Waters, are you all right? Who did this to you?"

"I think so," he said. "Get me out of this."

Cliff pulled a Swiss army knife from his pocket and sliced through the zip ties.

Waters pushed himself up into a sitting position, rolled onto his knees and staggered to his feet. "I have to go."

"Mr. Waters," Jenna said. "Where's your wife? Where's Trudy?"

Waters looked from Cliff to Jenna, his eyes widening. "Don't hurt her," he said. "Please, don't hurt her. She's been hurt enough."

"Where's your wife?" Jenna softened her tone. "We just want to talk to her."

He shook his head. "I tried to stop her. I tried to end the madness, but she wouldn't listen." His shoulders sagged, making him appear ten years older than he was. "She wouldn't listen. When I told her I had to fix this, she screamed at me and hit me with the cast iron skillet. I don't remember much after that until you two walked in."

"Mr. Waters, does your wife have my sister's baby?" Jenna asked.

The older man winced. "She hasn't been right

since the death of our son, Liam. She's so sad and angry. There's no consoling her. She's always been so kind and gentle. But lately…"

"Look at me." Cliff stepped up to the man, gripped his arms and forced him to look up. "Where is your wife?" he demanded in a clear, crisp tone.

"I don't know," he said. "Probably in the nursery."

"Where?"

"Second floor, first door on the left."

Before Cliff could stop her, Jenna raced out of the kitchen.

"Mr. Waters," Cliff said, "I want you to call 911 and ask them to send an ambulance. Can you do that?"

The man nodded, his eyes glazed, his hands shaking. "I can. I will."

Cliff started for the door leading out of the kitchen. Footsteps clattered on the staircase in the front foyer.

Thinking Trudy Waters might make a run for it, Cliff dashed out of the kitchen and down a hallway toward the front of the house,

When he emerged into the front foyer, the stairs were empty. The foyer was empty as well.

He took the steps two at a time to the top and hurried to the first door on the left, where voices sounded from within. Expecting the voices to be female, Cliff was shocked to hear a deeper, male voice say, "And you, a big deal FBI Agent led me right to my baby. All I had to do was follow you around. I would never have guessed this old bat took it. Thanks for saving me some time."

Cliff glanced into the nursery to find Mrs. Waters standing against the back wall beside a baby crib, an infant cradled in her arms. Baby Blakely.

To his right, Larry Sutton stood with his arm around Jenna's throat, a gun pressed to her temple.

"Now, give me the baby," Larry demanded. "It belongs to me."

Trudy Waters held the baby against her, rocking back and forth, humming softly.

"Tell her to give me the baby," Larry said. "Tell her, or I'll shoot you."

"It won't do any good," Jenna spoke softly. "She won't understand."

"What's wrong with the bitch? Can't she hear?" He raised his voice. "Hey, you! Give me the baby."

Trudy didn't even look up. She continued to sway and hum, her gaze fixed on the baby sleeping in her arms.

"Make her give me the kid," Larry said, his voice getting tighter, more desperate.

"If you try to take the baby away from her by force, she might drop it and injure it," Jenna reasoned. "What good is an injured baby to you, Larry? It won't bring as high a price with the adoption agency, will it?"

"Shut up. Shut the fuck up," he said and bumped

the pistol's muzzle against her temple. "If you can't get her to give me the kid, then I don't need you. I can just shoot you now and take the baby myself."

Cliff chose that moment to make his entrance, gun in hand, pointed at Larry. "I wouldn't do that," he said, his tone even and calm. "It's over. Your baby-selling days are done. Put down the gun and let Special Agent Jenkins go."

Sutton shook his head. "I don't know what you're talking about. That baby belongs to me."

"Just like the baby you made with Sandra Neal and sold for twenty thousand dollars?" Jenna said. "Are you going to sell your kids in Salt Lake City? Does Little Angels pay less for older children? How will your wife, Darlene, feel about that?

"How will you ever look her or your children in the eye, knowing you were selling babies for cash?" Jenna laughed. "Oh yeah, right, you have no sense of honor, no integrity. You're nothing but a human trafficker, a lying son-of-a-bitch who takes advantage of women and then steals their babies."

"Shut up," Larry yelled. "Shut the fuck up!" He nodded toward Cliff. "Get that baby from the crazy woman, or I'll put a bullet through your girlfriend's head."

"Jenna's right," Cliff said. "You are a lying son-of-a-bitch, the lowest of low-lifes who takes advantage of women and then steals their babies. If you want that baby, you'll have to get it yourself."

"You don't care much about your girl, do you?" Larry raised the gun a little higher. "I'll give you to the count of three."

Cliff's gut clenched. If he played the wrong hand, Jenna could die. "I don't respond to cowards who prey on women and children," Cliff said. "Now, are you going to put down your gun and go quietly, or am I going to have to shoot you? It'll make a big mess, your blood and brain matter scattering over everything around you."

Sirens wailed in the distance, getting louder as they approached the Waters' home.

"Don't add murder to your rap sheet," Jenna said. "You're not going to get out of this by hurting anyone else."

"I think I can get out of this," Larry said. "All I have to do is take a hostage. Oh, look, I already have one." He maneuvered her toward the door.

Jenna met Cliff's gaze and mouthed the words, *On three.*

Cliff's heart raced. Adrenaline thrummed through his veins, and he broke out in a sweat. The panic attack came on so fast that he wasn't ready.

Jenna's mouth formed the silent words, One… Two…Three.

Jenna went completely limp.

Her body's dead weight pulled Larry off balance. He lunged, tripped over her and fell. When he hit the floor, he rolled to his back and aimed for Cliff.

Fighting back the panic, Cliff lifted his arm, aimed at Larry and fired.

Two shots rang out.

Larry's bullet missed Cliff.

Cliff's bullet struck home, hitting Larry in the chest. The man's eyes widened. He clutched his chest, his breaths gurgling in his lungs.

Jenna straightened and moved toward Trudy and Baby Blakely. "Hey, Trudy, sweetie," she said softly. "Who've you got there?" She smiled and moved closer. "Can I see?"

Trudy half-turned away, a frown creasing her brown. "My baby."

"Yes, she is, and she's beautiful. I love holding babies. Don't you?"

Trudy's frown eased a little, and she turned back to Jenna. "She's so soft."

"Really? I love holding soft babies. Would you let me hold her for just a moment? It would make me so happy. You know, I lost a baby once. I miscarried. I cried so much I couldn't breathe. I would so love to hold a baby just once."

"Trudy, honey," David gently called out from the doorway. "Let your friend hold your baby for just a moment. She's really nice and thinks your baby is beautiful."

Trudy's brow wrinkled as she studied Jenna. "Okay, but only for a moment."

Jenna held out her arms and let Trudy lay the

baby in them. Once she had her, she studied what she could see of the baby's face and hands. Her breathing was steady, and she wasn't fussing.

A more thorough exam would have to be made by a pediatrician. For now, Jenna had to get her out of the room and away from Trudy.

David crossed to his wife's side and slid his arm around her. "Miss Jenna is going to take the baby back to her mother, where she belongs. Her real mother. She's been very worried about her baby."

Trudy shook her head from side to side, the motion getting more frenetic the more she shook. "No. That's my baby!" she wailed. "Please, don't take her away. I'll kill her," she yelled. "I'll kill her if she takes my baby away."

Cliff wrapped his arm around Jenna's shoulders and guided her toward the door, ever conscious of the woman growing more agitated by the minute.

"I'll kill her like I killed that old nurse who stole her out of the laundry cart when I went to get the truck. It was her, the only person I passed in the hall that night." Trudy's lips pulled back in a feral snarl. "She hid her in her own home. When I went to take her back, the old bat wanted to take my baby back to where she was born. I couldn't let that happen. No. She's mine."

Trudy looked up into her husband's eyes. "I couldn't let her take her back. She's your baby, too," she said, her voice softening. "I know you had an affair with that woman who gave birth to her. I hated her. But the baby is part of you. So, it's part of me. I love her. I want to hold her. To love her. I knew the baby was ours after you gave that whore your money. I planned to take her, stole the truck, the uniform, the ID card. I got our baby and then she was stolen from me!" Trudy clutched her husband's shirt. "Please, don't let them take her away. I can't lose another child. I can't."

Cliff and Jenna stopped short of the door, wanting to go but needing to know what drove this woman to do what she'd done,

"Sweetheart, she's not my baby. I didn't have an affair with her mother. I was trying to adopt her baby to provide her with a nice home. But she decided to keep her. Can you blame her? She's been so sad since her baby was taken."

"I can't do this again," she said, her eyes tearing and her mouth trembling.

Her husband pulled her into his arms and held her tightly.

She fought to get loose, pounding his chest. "Let me go," she cried. "They're taking my baby."

She broke free and staggered backward. When she tried to go to where Jenna stood, holding the baby, her husband stepped in front of her. "She's not your baby."

"She is!" Trudy screamed. "She has to be." She pounded his chest again.

David held her hands to keep her from hurting herself.

This time when she broke free, she flung herself away from him, crossed to the crib and yanked out a blanket. She tore it in half and flung it to the ground. Her hand swung at the little lamb lamp on the dresser, knocking it across the room and shattering the bulb.

"Trudy," her husband called out. "Please, sweetheart. You're going to hurt yourself."

"I don't care," she said. "Nothing matters anymore." She ran to the French doors, flung them open and ran out onto the balcony.

"No, Trudy!" David ran after his wife.

Cliff ran to help.

Before either man got to her, she climbed up on the banister and stood with her arms out wide.

David reached for her a moment too late.

Trudy leaned forward and plummeted to the ground.

Cliff and David leaned over the rail, then ran back through the nursery, down the stairs and outside to Trudy's twisted body.

When they reached Trudy, Cliff knew before he checked for a pulse that she was gone.

Police cars and an ambulance arrived.

Detective Schwope found Cliff and Jenna standing in the front entryway.

Jenna leaned the baby forward for him to see she was alive.

Blakely whimpered, stretched and slept.

The emergency medical technicians checked her over but insisted a pediatrician see her.

Jenna gave the detective an abbreviated version of what had happened and Trudy's confession. But she was eager to leave and get the baby to the hospital, where she could be checked over and fed.

"I'll file my report tomorrow," she told the detective. "Tonight, I want to make sure my niece is taken care of."

Cliff walked her out to the truck and held the baby while Jenna climbed into the back seat. Once she had her seatbelt buckled, he handed the baby up to her.

He stared up at her, his heart only now slowing to a normal pace. "You scared me."

She laughed. "You scared me."

He climbed up on the running board, leaned in and kissed her full on the mouth. "I'll be negotiating a lot more of that."

"Deal," she said and settled against the seat, a smile on her face, a baby in her arms.

Cliff climbed into the driver's seat and pulled away from the Waters' house. He shot a brief glance at her in the rearview mirror. "By the way, you... holding a baby...looks natural. Feels right."

She continued to smile. "Mmm. It does."

EPILOGUE

Two weeks later...

"Hurry up," Jenna urged. "Open another one. The sooner you're finished, the sooner we all get to eat."

Brittany laughed. "I'm doing the best I can. There are so many presents to open, I could use some help."

Cliff glanced around at the people gathered in the West Yellowstone Lodge. Men he'd served with on Navy SEAL teams and the women they loved all pitching in to give Brittany and Baby Blakely a good start on a new life.

The baby shower had been Jacob Stone's and his fiancée Kyla Russell's idea.

Jacob's father had offered Brittany a job at the lodge, helping with registration and event plan-ning. He'd made the job offer conditional on

Brittany going to college part-time online, working toward a degree in business management. He'd pay her tuition as long as she kept up her grades.

Along with working at the lodge, she had her own suite where she and Blakely had moved in.

Blakely had been declared none the worse for her bumpy start and had already gained half a pound, thriving on breast milk and love from the people on Cliff's new team.

Cliff had signed up with a PTSD therapist and met with him once a week, acknowledging he had issues and needed to work through them if he hoped to handle the panic attacks.

Jenna smiled at him across the room, her face glowing as she held Blakely while Brittany opened baby gifts.

The guys had welcomed him onto the Yellowstone team and introduced him to the area, its challenges and the beauty of the area.

Jenna worked out a deal with her higher headquarters to work half the week in Bozeman and the other half in West Yellowstone.

The spark he'd felt with Jenna continued to burn and grow. He'd give them a few more weeks of getting to know each other before he took the next step and asked her to marry him. Hell, they already lived together when they were in the same town. Marriage would just make it more official. Commitment. Meant a different four-letter word he could embrace for life.

LOVE.

He'd found the one for him and never wanted to let her go.

REMY

BAYOU BROTHERHOOD PROTECTORS
BOOK #1

New York Times & *USA Today*
Bestselling Author

ELLE JAMES

REMY

Bayou
BROTHERHOOD PROTECTORS

New York Times & USA Today Bestselling Author
ELLE JAMES

CHAPTER 1

WITH THE SUN dipping over the treetops and dusk settling beneath the boughs of the cypress trees, Deputy Shelby Taylor checked her watch. It would be dark before long. She should be turning around and heading back to the town of Bayou Mambaloa.

Named after the bayou on the edge of which it perched, the town was Shelby's home, where she'd been born and raised. But for a seven-year break, she'd lived in that small town all of her life.

So many young people left Bayou Mambaloa as soon as they turned eighteen. Many went to college or left for employment in New Orleans, Baton Rouge, Houston or some other city. Good-paying jobs were scarce in Bayou Mambaloa unless you were a fishing guide or the owner of a bed and breakfast. The primary industries keeping the town alive were tourism and fishing.

Thankfully, between the two of them, there was enough work for the small town to thrive for at least nine months of the year. The three months of cooler weather gave the residents time to regroup, restock, paint and get ready for the busy part of the year.

As small as Bayou Mambaloa was, it had an inordinate amount of crime per capita. Thus necessitating a sheriff's department and sheriff's deputies, who worked the 911 dispatch calls, responding to everything from rogue alligators in residential pools to drug smuggling.

Shelby sighed. Having grown up on the bayou, she knew her way around on land and in the water.

Her father had always wanted a boy. When all her mother had produced was Shelby and her sister, he hadn't let that slow him down. A fishing guide, her father had taken her out fishing nearly three-hundred-and-sixty-five days of the year, allowing her to steer whatever watercraft he had at the time—pirogues, canoes, bass boats, Jon boats and even an airboat.

Whenever a call came needing someone to get out on the bayou, her name was first on the list. She had to admit that she preferred patrolling in a boat versus in one of the SUVs in the department's fleet. Still, there were so many tributaries, islands, twists and turns in the bayou that if smugglers hid there, they'd be hard to find, even for Shelby.

She'd been on the water since seven o'clock that

morning after an anonymous caller had reported seeing two men on an airboat offloading several wooden crates onto an island in the bayou.

The report came on the heels of a heads-up from a Narcotics Detective with the Louisiana State Police's Criminal Investigations Division.

An informant had said that a drug cartel had set up shop in or near Bayou Mambaloa. The parish Sheriff's Department was to report anything they might find that was suspicious or indicative of drug running in their area.

Because the tip had been anonymous, Sheriff Bergeron had sent Shelby out to investigate and report her findings. She was not to engage, just mark the spot with her GPS and get that information back as soon as possible.

The caller had given a general location, which could have included any number of islands.

Shelby had circled at least ten islands during the day, walked the length of half of them and found nothing.

The only time she'd returned to Marcelle's Marina had been to fill the boat's gas tank and grab a sandwich and more water. At that time, she'd checked in with Sheriff Bergeron. He hadn't had any more calls and hadn't heard from CID. With nothing pressing going on elsewhere in the parish, he'd had Shelby continue her search.

Normally, any chance to get out of the patrol car

and on the water was heaven for Shelby. Not that day. Oppressive, late summer heat bore down on her all day. With humidity at ninety-seven percent, she'd started sweating at eight in the morning, consumed a gallon of water and was completely drenched.

She wished it would go ahead and rain to wash away the stench of her perspiration. Maybe, in the process, the rain would lower the temperature to less than hell's fiery inferno.

She passed a weathered fishing shack and sighed as she read the fading sign painted in blue letters— The Later Gator Fishing Hut. She released the throttle and let the skiff float slowly by.

A rush of memories flooded through her, bringing a sad smile to her lips. Less than a month ago, she'd spent a stormy night in that shack with a man she'd harbored a school-girl crush on for over twenty years.

She'd insisted it would only be a one-night stand they'd both walk away from with no regrets. She didn't regret that night or making love to the man. It had been an amazing night, and the sex had been better than she'd ever dreamed it could be.

However, despite her reassurances to him, she'd come away with one regret.

It had only been one night.

She wanted more.

But that wasn't to be. He'd gone on to the job waiting for him in Montana, never looking back.

He'd left Bayou Mambaloa twenty years ago. His short visit hadn't been enough to bring him back for good.

She hadn't been enough to make him want to stay.

Shelby gave the motor a surge of gas, sending the skiff away from the hut, but her memories followed. Focusing on the waterway ahead, she tried to banish the man and the memories from her thoughts.

By the time she headed back to Marcelle's Marina, the heat had taken its toll. She was tired, cranky and not at her best.

Shelby almost missed the airboat parked in an inlet half-hidden among the drooping boughs of a cypress tree. If movement out of the corner of her eye hadn't caught her attention, she would have driven her boat past without noting the coordinates.

When she turned, she spotted two men climbing aboard an airboat filled with wooden crates.

At the same moment, the taller one of the two men spotted her, grabbed the other man's arm and pointed in her direction.

"Fuck," Shelby muttered and fumbled to capture the coordinates with her cell phone, knowing she wasn't supposed to engage. If these were truly drug smugglers, they would be heavily armed.

The tall man pulled a handgun out of his waistband, aimed at Shelby and fired.

As soon as the gun came out, Shelby ducked.

Though it missed her, the bullet hit the side of her boat.

She dropped her cell phone, hit the throttle and sent the skiff powering through the bayou as fast as the outboard motor would take her.

Another shot rang out over the sound of the engine. The bullet glanced off the top of the motor, cracking the casing, but the engine roared on.

Her heart pounding like a snare drum at a rock concert, Shelby sped through the water, spun around fields of tall marsh grass, hunkering low while hoping she would disappear from their sight long enough to lose herself in the bayou.

For a moment, she dared believe she'd succeeded as she skimmed past a long stretch of marsh grass. She raised her head to peer over the vegetation, looking back in the direction of the two men.

To her immediate right, bright headlights dispelled the dusky darkness as the airboat cleaved a path through the marsh grass, blasting toward her.

Her skiff, with its outboard motor, was no match for the other craft. She had to steer around marsh grass or risk getting her propeller tangled, which meant zig-zagging through the bayou to avoid vegetation.

Not the airboat. Instead of going around, it cut through the field of grass, barreling straight for Shelby in her skiff.

She spun the bow to the left, but not soon enough to avoid the collision.

The larger airboat rammed into the front of the small skiff. The force of the blow launched the skiff into the air.

Shelby was thrown into the water and sank into darkness to the silty floor of the bayou.

As she scrambled to get her bearings and struggled to swim to the surface, the skiff came down hard over her. If not for the water's surface breaking the boat's fall, it would have crushed her and broken her neck. Instead, the hard metal smacked her hard, sending her back down into the silt. Her lungs burned, and her vision blurred.

Her mind numbing, she had only one thought.

Air.

The black water of the bayou dragged at her clothing. The silt at her feet sucked her deeper.

Her head spun, and pain throbbed through her skull. She used every last ounce of strength and consciousness and pushed her booted feet into the silt, sending herself upward. As she surfaced, her head hit something hard, sending her back beneath the water before she could fill her lungs.

Shelby surfaced a second time, her cheek scraping the side of something as she breached the surface and sucked in a deep breath.

She blinked. Were her eyes even open? The darkness was so complete she wondered for a second if the blow making her head throb and her thoughts blur had blinded her. Or was this how it felt to be dead?

She raised her hand to touch the object that had scraped her cheek. Metal. In the back of her mind, she knew she was still in the boat, but it was upside-down. The metal in front of her was the bench she'd been seated on moments before. She wrapped her fingers around the bench to keep her head above water in the air pocket between the bottom of the boat and the bayou's surface.

A whirring sound moved away and then returned, growing louder the closer it came to the inverted skiff. It slowed as it approached. Then metal clanked against metal, and the skiff lurched, the bow dipping lower into the water.

Still holding onto the bench, Shelby's murky brain registered danger. She held on tightly to the bench as the skiff was pushed through the water.

The whir outside increased along with the sound of metal scraping on metal. The front end of the skiff dipped low in the water, dipping the hull lower. Soon, Shelby's head touched the bottom of the boat, and her nose barely cleared the surface.

Whatever was moving the skiff was forcing it deeper.

Shelby had to get out from beneath the boat or drown. Tipping her head back, she breathed in a last breath, released the bench and grabbed for the side of the skiff. She pulled herself toward the edge, ducked beneath it and swam as hard as she could, her efforts jerky, her clothes weighing her down. She couldn't see her hands in front of her, and her lungs screamed for air.

When she thought she couldn't go another inch further, her hands bumped into stalks. She wrapped her fingers around them and pulled herself between them, snaking her way into a forest of reeds. Once her feet bumped against them, she lifted her head above the water and sucked in air. For a moment, the darkness wasn't as dark; the thickening dusk and the glow of headlights gave her just enough light to make out the dark strands of marsh grass surrounding her.

The whirring sound was behind her. Metal-on-metal screeches pierced the air, moving toward her. The grass stalks bent, touching her feet.

In a burst of adrenaline, Shelby ducked beneath the water and threaded her way deeper into the marsh. She moved as fast as she could to get away from the looming hulk of the skiff, plowing toward her through the marsh, pushing the skiff beneath it.

The adrenaline and her strength waning, she barely stayed ahead of the skiff being bull-dozed through the grass.

Shelby surfaced for air, so tired she barely had the energy to breathe. It would be so much easier to die.

Holding onto several stalks, she turned to face her death.

The engine cut off. Two lights shined out over the marsh. Another light blinked to life, the beam sweeping over the skiff's hull and the surrounding area.

As the beam neared Shelby, she sank beneath the surface and shifted the reeds enough to cover her head. The beam shone across her position.

Shelby froze. For a long moment, the ray held steady. If it didn't move on soon, she'd be forced to surface to breathe.

When she thought her lungs would burst, the beam shifted past.

Shelby tilted her head back, let her nose and mouth rise to the surface and breathed in.

The light swept back her way so fast she didn't have time to duck lower. Shelby stiffened, her pulse pounding through her veins and throbbing in her head.

Before the light reached her, it snapped off.

She dared to raise her head out of the water enough to clear her ears.

"She has to be dead," a voice said.

Through the reeds, Shelby could just make out two silhouettes between the headlights of the airboat.

"We need to flip the skiff and make sure," a lower voice said.

"I'm not getting in that water to flip no skiff. I saw four alligators earlier."

"You don't see them now," the man with the lower voice argued.

"Exactly why I'm not getting in the water. You don't know where they are in the dark. If you want to check, you get in."

After a pause, the man with the deep voice said. "You're right. Alligators are sneaky bastards."

"Damn right," his partner agreed. "Besides, that woman's dead."

"And if she's not?"

The flashlight blinked on again, the beam directed at the skiff. "She'd better be," the guy with the higher voice said. "Do you see the lettering on the side of that boat?"

"S-h-e-r…" Low-voice man spoke each letter out loud and then paused.

"It spells sheriff," the other guy finished.

"Fuck," low-voice man swore. "We killed a goddamn sheriff?"

"Yeah." The flashlight blinked off. "Let's get the fuck out of here."

The airboat engine revved, and the huge fan on the back of the craft whirred to life. The airboat backed off the skiff and turned, the lights sweeping over Shelby's position.

She sank below the water's surface, the sound of the airboat rumbling in her ears.

Soon, the sound faded.

Shelby bobbed to the surface. The airboat was

gone, and with it, the bright lights. Clouds scudded across the night sky, alternately blocking and revealing a fingernail moon. When it wasn't shrouded in clouds, it glowed softly, turning the inky black into indigo blue.

Her strength waning and her vision fading in and out of a gray mist, Shelby couldn't think past the throbbing in her head.

Out of the haze, the man's comment about alligators surfaced.

She hadn't escaped death by drowning only to become dinner to a hungry reptile.

Somehow, she managed to push her way back through the marsh grass to the mangled hull of the skiff, now crushed low and only a couple of inches above the water's surface. Shelby tried to pull herself up onto the side of the slick metal hull. With nothing to grab hold of, she had no leverage, nor did she have the strength.

Swimming around to the stern, she stepped onto the motionless propeller. With her last ounce of strength and energy, she pushed upward and flopped her body onto the hull. Her forehead bounced against the metal, sending a sharp pain through her already aching head.

Though the clouds chose that moment to clear and let the moon shine down on the bayou, Shelby succumbed to darkness.

ABOUT THE AUTHOR

ELLE JAMES also writing as MYLA JACKSON is a *New York Times* and *USA Today* Bestselling author of books including cowboys, intrigues and paranormal adventures that keep her readers on the edges of their seats. When she's not at her computer, she's traveling, snow skiing, boating, or riding her ATV, dreaming up new stories. Learn more about Elle James at www.ellejames.com

Website | Facebook | Twitter | GoodReads | Newsletter | BookBub | Amazon

Or visit her alter ego Myla Jackson at mylajackson.com
Website | Facebook | Twitter | Newsletter

Follow Me!
www.ellejames.com
ellejamesauthor@gmail.com

ALSO BY ELLE JAMES

Bayou Brotherhood Protectors

Remy (#1)

Gerard (#2)

Lucas (#3)

Beau (#4)

Rafael (#5)

Valentin (#6)

Landry (#7)

Simon (#8)

Maurice (#9)

Jacques (#10)

Brotherhood Protectors Yellowstone

Saving Kyla (#1)

Saving Chelsea (#2)

Saving Amanda (#3)

Saving Liliana (#4)

Saving Breely (#5)

Saving Savvie (#6)

Saving Jenna (#7)

Saving Peyton (#8)

Brotherhood Protectors Colorado

SEAL Salvation (#1)

Rocky Mountain Rescue (#2)

Ranger Redemption (#3)

Tactical Takeover (#4)

Colorado Conspiracy (#5)

Rocky Mountain Madness (#6)

Free Fall (#7)

Colorado Cold Case (#8)

Fool's Folly (#9)

Colorado Free Rein (#10)

Rocky Mountain Venom (#11)

High Country Hero (#12)

Brotherhood Protectors

Montana SEAL (#1)

Bride Protector SEAL (#2)

Montana D-Force (#3)

Cowboy D-Force (#4)

Montana Ranger (#5)

Montana Dog Soldier (#6)

Montana SEAL Daddy (#7)

Montana Ranger's Wedding Vow (#8)

Montana SEAL Undercover Daddy (#9)

Cape Cod SEAL Rescue (#10)

Montana SEAL Friendly Fire (#11)

Montana SEAL's Mail-Order Bride (#12)

SEAL Justice (#13)

Ranger Creed (#14)

Delta Force Rescue (#15)

Dog Days of Christmas (#16)

Montana Rescue (#17)

Montana Ranger Returns (#18)

Hot SEAL Salty Dog (SEALs in Paradise)

Hot SEAL,Hawaiian Nights (SEALs in Paradise)

Hot SEAL Bachelor Party (SEALs in Paradise)

Hot SEAL, Independence Day (SEALs in Paradise)

Brotherhood Protectors Boxed Set 1

Brotherhood Protectors Boxed Set 2

Brotherhood Protectors Boxed Set 3

Brotherhood Protectors Boxed Set 4

Brotherhood Protectors Boxed Set 5

Brotherhood Protectors Boxed Set 6

Shadow Assassin

Iron Horse Legacy

Soldier's Duty (#1)

Ranger's Baby (#2)

Marine's Promise (#3)

SEAL's Vow (#4)

Warrior's Resolve (#5)

Drake (#6)

Grimm (#7)

Murdock (#8)

Utah (#9)

Judge (#10)

Delta Force Strong

Ivy's Delta (Delta Force 3 Crossover)

Breaking Silence (#1)

Breaking Rules (#2)

Breaking Away (#3)

Breaking Free (#4)

Breaking Hearts (#5)

Breaking Ties (#6)

Breaking Point (#7)

Breaking Dawn (#8)

Breaking Promises (#9)

Hearts & Heroes Series

Wyatt's War (#1)

Mack's Witness (#2)

Ronin's Return (#3)

Sam's Surrender (#4)

Love & War (#4)

Billionaire Online Dating Service
The Billionaire Husband Test (#1)
The Billionaire Cinderella Test (#2)
The Billionaire Bride Test (#3)
The Billionaire Daddy Test (#4)
The Billionaire Matchmaker Test (#5)
The Billionaire Glitch Date (#6)
The Billionaire Perfect Date (#7) coming soon
The Billionaire Replacement Date (#8) coming soon
The Billionaire Wedding Date (#9) coming soon

Cajun Magic Mystery Series
Voodoo on the Bayou (#1)
Voodoo for Two (#2)
Deja Voodoo (#3)
Cajun Magic Mysteries Books 1-3

The Outriders
Homicide at Whiskey Gulch (#1)
Hideout at Whiskey Gulch (#2)
Held Hostage at Whiskey Gulch (#3)
Setup at Whiskey Gulch (#4)
Missing Witness at Whiskey Gulch (#5)

Navy SEAL Captive

Navy SEAL To Die For

Navy SEAL Six Pack

Devil's Shroud Series

Deadly Reckoning (#1)

Deadly Engagement (#2)

Deadly Liaisons (#3)

Deadly Allure (#4)

Deadly Obsession (#5)

Deadly Fall (#6)

Covert Cowboys Inc Series

Triggered (#1)

Taking Aim (#2)

Bodyguard Under Fire (#3)

Cowboy Resurrected (#4)

Navy SEAL Justice (#5)

Navy SEAL Newlywed (#6)

High Country Hideout (#7)

Clandestine Christmas (#8)

Thunder Horse Series

Hostage to Thunder Horse (#1)

Thunder Horse Heritage (#2)

Thunder Horse Redemption (#3)

Christmas at Thunder Horse Ranch (#4)

Demon Series

Hot Demon Nights (#1)

Demon's Embrace (#2)

Tempting the Demon (#3)

Lords of the Underworld

Witch's Initiation (#1)

Witch's Seduction (#2)

The Witch's Desire (#3)

Possessing the Witch (#4)

Stealth Operations Specialists (SOS)

Nick of Time

Alaskan Fantasy

Boys Behaving Badly Anthologies

Rogues (#1)

Blue Collar (#2)

Pirates (#3)

Stranded (#4)

First Responder (#5)

Silver Soldier's (#6)

Blown Away

Warrior's Conquest

Enslaved by the Viking Short Story

Conquests

Smokin' Hot Firemen

Protecting the Colton Bride

Protecting the Colton Bride & Colton's Cowboy Code

Heir to Murder

Secret Service Rescue

High Octane Heroes

Haunted

Engaged with the Boss

Cowboy Brigade

Time Raiders: The Whisper

Bundle of Trouble

Killer Body

Operation XOXO

An Unexpected Clue

Baby Bling

Under Suspicion, With Child

Texas-Size Secrets

Cowboy Sanctuary

Lakota Baby

Dakota Meltdown

Beneath the Texas Moon

Made in the USA
Las Vegas, NV
16 September 2024

95352799R00144